COMPANY OF COWARDS

D1568752

Also by Jack Schaefer

COMPANY OF COWARDS

JACK SCHAEFER

University of New Mexico Press | Albuquerque

Library of Congress Cataloging-in-Publication Data
Names: Schaefer, Jack, 1907–1991, author.
Title: Company of Cowards / Jack Schaefer.
Description: University of New Mexico Press edition. |
Albuquerque : University of New Mexico Press, 2017.
Identifiers: LCCN 2017004058| ISBN 9780826358639 (softcover : acid-free paper) |
ISBN 9780826358646 (e-book)
Subjects: LCSH: United States—History—Civil War, 1861-1865—Fiction. |
GSAFD: Historical fiction.
Classification: LCC PS3537.C223 C66 2017 | DDC 813/.54—dc23 LC record
available at https://lccn.loc.gov/2017004058

Cover art: *Civil War Scene,*
by Paul Philippoteaux (1846–1923), oil on canvas, 32 ¼ x 58 in.
Courtesy of Godel & Co., Inc., NYC
Designed by Catherine Leonardo
Composed in Adobe Jenson Pro 11/15
Display font is Adobe Jenson Pro and Avenir

This one for Hank

May, 1864. In the dark, tangled woodland south of the Rapidan, where second-growth pine and matted vines and underbrush clogged movement and clouded vision, the Army of the Potomac and the Army of Northern Virginia were locked in the deadly, unearthly embrace of the Battle of the Wilderness. This was the brutal beginning of the long, last, grinding ordeal that would lead to Appomattox Court House. That was not known then. The past hung heavy over the immediate present. Again and again the Army of the Potomac had started on the road to Richmond only to have its driving power blunted and broken against Confederate courage and the daring shining integrity of Robert E. Lee. The list of commanders failing and being replaced had lengthened: Scott and McClellan and Pope and Burnside and Hooker and Meade. The best that could be said was that Meade had held firm at Gettysburg.

Now the Army of the Potomac was moving again under a stubby, stubborn little man from out of the west named Grant who would fight and fight and fight again until the brute weight of superior numbers and resources would grind out a final victory. He had swung left of Lee's long fortified line and crossed the

Rapidan and headed south through that strange, murky wood-land, hoping to strike on through and draw Lee down to the open ground beyond before coming to battle-grip—and Lee had driven slashing in from the side to grapple with him there in the Wilderness.

All that is nailed down in history, described and redescribed and argued and analyzed in volumes enough to fill a large library. Why worry it again and in words that can never recapture the harsh, stinging reality of the bitterest, bloodiest fighting ever to torment American soil?

Because this is not a story of the Civil War. It is the story of a man who followed his own peculiar trail out of that war and on to his own peculiar victory. And of the queer, crippled, unrecorded company that went with him.

His name was Jared Heath. It stands, in firm slanting script, on the first line of the first page of a small, leather-laced account book in which he kept an intermittent journal of events. *Jared Heath, 12th Massachusetts Volunteers.* And beneath it the first entry: *1861, May 11. Answered the call to the colors.*

The date there indicates that the call he was answering was Lincoln's appeal issued a few days earlier for 42,000 men to serve for three years or the duration of the war. No matter that no one thought then the war would last more than a few months. His enlistment made him one of the regulars, the hard core of duration men who held the Union forces together and served on while the three-month and the six-month and the one-year men came and went and the draft was born of necessity and was corrupted by the bounty and substitute evils that accompanied it. He was a regular, a three-year man, and it was natural he should be. He was the third Jared Heath in direct line to wear an American uniform.

His grandfather, who brought the name to this country, had served under Washington himself, one of the ragged continentals who marched and endured and fought through the weary years to Yorktown and saw the United States come into being. The old man, still living when this Jared Heath was a boy, stern of bearded face, erect as a ramrod to the last, wore again his old revolutionary uniform and shouldered again his old revolutionary musket to lead the local Fourth of July parades. He had little to say, probably because he had done much. His deeds, part of a heroic history, acquiring the mystic glow of an accomplished glory, spoke for him and gave the family a distinction in the local community that had pleasant, social overtones and was good for the family business.

The father, second of the name, with the same sternness of face, the same and perhaps somewhat self-conscious erectness of bearing, had much to say, perhaps too much, perhaps too frequent and labored a harping. He must have felt overshadowed by the presence and later the memory of the old man. His own war had, in effect, cheated him. Massachusetts and the rest of New England had no relish for the War of 1812, did not want it, even refused to supply troops when Congress voted the declaration and called for militia. Indignant, he tried to organize rallies and made speeches and at last tramped over to New York State and enlisted there.

He was with the army dispatched to take the British posts across the Niagara River in Canada. When part of the army had crossed, the New York troops refused to leave New York soil. No doubt indignant again, held there in the immobile ranks, he saw those who had crossed beaten by the British and driven back to the river's edge and ingloriously captured. Then the war was over and not once had he marched into actual battle. But he had been ready to march. In time, in his talk—he married late and had it well worked out by then—he could cast a glow of glory over what he had done. In the words worn by repetition and echoed in his son's journal, he had answered the call to the colors.

So this Jared Heath, third of the name, unhesitating, with the weight of two older generations on his square-set shoulders and gallantly unaware of that weight, answered Lincoln's call, among the first in his county, setting an example as such a man should. His mother, frail, never fully recovered from a lingering childbed sickness, bore up well and set to work sewing extra linen for him. His brother, still in knee pants, regarded him with increased envy and admiration. His father talked more than ever, working through familiar tales of two wars. It was all as it should be. He was no raw youngster bowled over by band-playing and flag-waving and the thought of parading in uniform. He was a man answering the call to the colors. Twenty-four at the time, already a partner in the family foundry, solid and compact and competent in mind and body, a staunch Unionist, he knew what he was doing and why. His father's patriotic references to following the old flag and upholding the family tradition may have seemed to him excessive but certainly not off-key. He was, as the recruiting officer remarked and as his father repeated in later letters, excellent soldier material, the kind of man the country needed to whip the rebels into swift submission.

There were others like him scattered through those first hurriedly assembled regiments and it was fortunate there were when the Union forces all but collapsed under the initial impact of rebel strength and determination. What set him apart, if anything could be said to set him apart at the time, was a slight, rarely noticed, exaggeration of another aspect of his New England heritage, the proverbial Yankee stubbornness of mind.

The record of the next three years is all there in his journal, the facts at least, simple and direct, with occasional flashes suggesting thoughts behind them. Those were the days, in the first stage of the war, when newly recruited regiments elected their own line officers. He had his lieutenant's bar within the week. As a lieutenant he marched out to First Bull Run. The entry on that is brief, blunt: *Unable to rally the men. Forced to retreat.* And one of the rare flashes: *Like Grandpa at Brandywine.*

That was his baptism in battle, not really a battle, a retreat becoming a rout, but one in which panic did not push him as it did so many others, a test he took well, in the tradition—like Grandpa at Brandywine.

Thereafter, for a long stretch, he was in a sense out of the war, out of the fighting, stranded in garrison duty close to Washington. Lincoln and the Cabinet, shaken by the defeat, pressured too by Congress, insisted that a strong screen of troops be maintained around the city. That was pleasant duty, in snug quarters, with regular meals and a round of parties to attend and the actual fighting relatively far away. But it was not for that a Jared Heath had answered the call to the colors. Perhaps he felt that his war too was cheating him. There is an entry made after a party at some unnamed colonel's quarters, where battles were won in words over a good dinner and future victory toasted in wine: *This is no way to win a war.* And there are a few shrewd comments on the generals in the field. When the peninsular campaign, striking toward Richmond up the land neck between the James and York Rivers, fizzled out in weary withdrawal and the reports trickled into Washington, he hit it in a single short sentence: *McClellan is not the man.*

Then Antietam finished McClellan and Fredericksburg finished Burnside and Hooker took over and dreamed his personal dream of crushing Lee and some of the garrison troops were pulled away from Washington to augment his field force. Lieutenant Jared Heath was back in the war, marching toward Chancellorsville. But not into battle. Close enough to hear it, to smell it, to see some of it. He was with the brigades held back by Hooker, unused out of some strange caution or indecision in the man even when his whole right wing was crumpled by Stonewall Jackson's flank assault and Lee was battering him back in defeat. The entry on that is one of the briefest: *Kept out of it.* Then another of the flashes: *Almost like Father up in New York.* Followed by another, right again as rain: *Hooker is through. Fights like a man with one hand tied.*

Nothing remarkable, nothing unusual in all that. The conviction had long been spreading through the Army of the Potomac, through the men in the ranks and the line officers, that politics and suspicion and confusion and downright stupidity in the high places, reaching perhaps even to the presidency and certainly to the Cabinet, were depriving them of the leadership they deserved or at least needed. The letters and diaries of other men in that army, men who like this Jared Heath were alert and used their minds some, run much the same. It was part of the prolonged, shaking-down process, the shift from expectation of a swift, gallant, flag-waving suppression of the rebellion to some understanding of the ordeal ahead, some realization that this war would be won only by a bitter struggle of endurance.

Then Meade was in command and Lee was smashing north into Pennsylvania and Lieutenant Jared Heath was marching toward Gettysburg. He won his captaincy there, breveted on the field after holding his platoon firm in the face of repeated assaults. The entry simply states the facts. And adds: *Wrote Father about it.* Back home in Massachusetts his father must have been busy polishing another battle account for his stock of family tales.

Yes, it is all there, the record of the three years following his enlistment, the pertinent facts fitting the third Jared Heath into his place in his war, right up to the start of the last long campaign southward under Grant, the entry on that hurriedly written, probably during a brief rest halt: *Crossed the Rapidan at Germanna Ford. Moving toward Wilderness Tavern.* It is the record of a good soldier, steady and intelligent, alert to what he was doing and why, stiffening like those of his breed around him to the long hard task as its measure began to unfold, consciously and perhaps proudly upholding a family tradition—a man, you would say, who would see it through as his grandfather had done before him.

But he did not see it through.

Something is missing, or hidden, or never committed to paper. The record revealed by that journal was heading toward a moment that would repudiate it. Was there a slow change in the man of which he himself was unaware? Was it Gettysburg, on whose haunted battlefield the high-bannered pageantry and gallantry of old-style, time-honored warfare rose to its final moment and died away forever in the crumpled crushed glory of Pickett's charge, that started a corrosive unconscious change in him? Or was there no change at all but a sudden revealing of essential character, of his own individual unique segment of mortality laid raw and bare at last?

The man who wrote the first entry, echoing the family phrase, was in all seeming circumstance young, confident, quite certain he was stepping out on the glory road that would lead to a quick color-ful quenching of the rebellion. The man who wrote the final entry, three years later almost to the day, had aged in more than time and the normal rigors of war, most of it in the last few days. He had forsaken the glory road. The quenching of the rebellion no longer touched him. He was looking down another and far different road and all that counted was the far lonely question of his own individual integrity.

It is all over—Why?

And again, in strokes tearing the page: *Why?*

If a full answer were ever found, only Jared Heath himself could have been certain and he never spoke of it, not even in the later years, long after the war, when settlement spread out toward his small homestead ranch in northern New Mexico and he mingled more with neighbors and the garrulousness of age crept on him. He would talk readily enough, in those last years, when prompted to it, of the distant days in the Wilderness and after, speaking of himself and events with a strange and strangely impressive detachment, a remoteness, almost an indifference, as if all that too no longer touched him and he had pushed beyond into another existence. But he never spoke of what those events had meant to him, what meaning he had wrung out of them. That was his alone. All that can be done is to tell what happened there in the Wilderness and what followed.

One

It was midmorning when they forded the river. Back in the night a cavalry regiment had slipped across and cleared away the few rebel pickets. In the first morning hours a division of cavalry had crossed as advance guard and gone up the curving road to disappear into the dim woodland beyond. Now the infantry, broken out of camps and assembled in marching order, were moving, the 12th Massachusetts among them, splashing through the ford and regrouping on the other side and heading up and on into the Wilderness. Eastward, down the river a few miles at Ely's Ford, Hooker's old crossing, more of the army was in motion, marching southward in almost parallel line along the battle-scarred road to Chancellorsville. And in the reaches behind both fords the men of the artillery brigades and of the great lumbering canvas-topped supply trains were harnessing and wheeling into formation to follow.

There was a brightness that spring day in the valley they were leaving, a golden mist of sunlight shimmering on the dogwood and the early flowers almost hidden in the fresh growing grasses. There was joking among the men and comments ran along the marching column, but subdued, lacking the lightness of the start of other campaigns under jauntier more flamboyant commanders. This was a bigger, grimmer, tougher army, taking its tone from the stubby stubborn little man who would use it, not as a sword, with skill, flashing in supple action, but as a hammer pounding out victory over lesser forces at whatever cost. Despite the myriad sounds of masses of men and battle equipment in movement, a muffled hush hung over the long lines. They moved out of the brightness, looking back and then facing forward, into the dark woodland.

All that day and all went well. They moved southward down the Germanna Road, the tangled murky growth thickening on either side, and went into bivouac in the heart of the Wilderness, the infantry near the old abandoned stage station called Wilderness Tavern at the crossroads where the Orange Turnpike came in from the west, the cavalry on ahead near the old landmark known as Tapp Farm where the Orange Plank Road also came in from the west. Not a sound, not a sight of rebel activity along the way. Nothing to mar the evening relaxation of rest and campaign rations after a dreary plodding through an almost deserted land where only a few weedy clearings and tumbledown shacks stood against the encroaching matted growth. Yet an uneasy apprehension clung to the men around their small shared campfires. They knew that off to the west where those two side roads, the only passable routes, ran silent and somehow ominous in their silence into the last light of the dying sun, were Robert E. Lee and the Army of Northern Virginia. Perhaps this new general Grant was stealing a march on old Marse Bob at last. But many had tried and no one yet had stolen a march on that great legendary man in gray.

The first darkness of night held thick over the sprawling infantry encampment. No neat orderly arrangement here, not in this forbidden resistant wilderness cut by hidden ravines and clogged with its tangled growth. The various units lay as the land itself let them, roughly along the road but off it to keep it clear. A fire, flaring in brief flame as fresh fuel was applied, might be invisible only a few yards away or simply glimpsed fitfully through the underbrush. A dark ghostly glimmering hung under the low branches of the stunted pines, fading as fires died and soldiers crept under their slanted dog tents to clutch at uneasy sleep.

Colonel Goddard's V-topped tent, seeming unnaturally large in its recently cleared small space under the trees, gave off a weird spotty faint glow through its worn old canvas from the lit candles within. The tent flaps parted and Major Moody appeared, followed by Captains Heath and Clemmons, pausing in respectful silence as the colonel himself stepped out behind them. Tall, wide-mustached, military correctness in every detail, Colonel Goddard peered at the others in the outer darkness. "That's it, gentlemen," he said. "Goodnight and get some rest." The tent flaps fell softly into place as he returned inside.

Captain Clemmons pulled a cigar from a pocket and stooped his long rangy shape to pick up an ember from the remains of a small fire. He drew in deeply and let the smoke out in two streamers through his nose. "Not exactly the most direct route to Richmond," he said.

Captain Jared Heath looked off westward through the trees. His voice had a faint edge of irritation. "There's a little something in the way over there. Its name is Lee."

"So we make a run around him," said Captain Clemmons. "So we hope to pull him out where we want him. When we ought to go down the bay by boat and strike up the peninsula. Open country there for maneuvers. A straightaway to Richmond. McClellan had the right idea."

Captain Heath turned toward him. "And where is McClellan now?"

"Damn it, Heath must you always be so practical? Always have the answers, don't you?" Captain Clemmons held up his cigar and flicked at the tiny ash end with the forefinger of the other hand. "Well, it'll be a long night and a longer tomorrow." He swung away and disappeared into the darkness toward his own quarters.

"Easy, Jared." Major Moody's voice came softly from his position a few feet away. Lean, gray-haired, slightly stooped, he carried the tired patience of a man in whom ambition had dwindled, who had found his niche and was content with it. He stepped forward and put a hand on Captain Heath's shoulder. "You know Clemmons. Talks first and thinks afterwards." He too moved off into the darkness.

Head down, watching for trailing vines, Captain Heath followed the bare trace of a path around clumped underbrush toward his own tent, emerging into the flickering circle of light from a fire burning to one side of it. Out of shadow appeared two figures, Lieutenants Beatty and Wilkeson. They waited for him to speak.

"No change," he said. "Straight on in the morning. By tomorrow night we ought to be about out of this confounded forest."

"Right, sir," said Lieutenant Beatty, young, eager, new to the rank. "A good thing, sir. This is no place to run into a fight."

Faintly, drifting through the trees to them from a group of men lingering around a fire some twenty yards away, came a voice. "Hey, Hank. Give us that prayer you was talking of."

Slowly, drawling, deliberately deepened, gently mocking, another voice drifted through the low-branched darkness:

Our Father who art in Washington,
Uncle Abraham be Thy name . . .

It paused and in the pause Lieutenant Wilkeson stiffened. "Blasphemous!" he said in a hushed shocked whisper. "Oughtn't I go break it up, sir?"

"No!" Captain Heath's voice, held low, had an irritated snap. "It's no more blasphemous than war itself. And probably just as necessary. Let them alone."

Lieutenant Wilkeson, thickset, full-bearded, middle-aged, ever aware of his seniority in years, stiffened further, withdrawing into the aloofness of his own self-righteousness. And deep-toned, gently mocking, the distant voice came again:

Thy will be done at the South as at the North.
Give us this day our daily ration
Of crackers, salt horse and pork.
Forgive us our shortcomings
As we forgive our Quartermaster.
For thine is the power,
The soldiers and the niggers,
For the space of three years.
Amen.

Silence. Abruptly Captain Heath broke it, turning toward the two lieutenants. "That's all. We'll be pulling out early in the morning." He watched the two, dismissed, stride into the enveloping darkness. Quietly, picking his way, he moved toward the lingering group around the dying fire. Invisible in the deeper dark by a low pine, he watched as the men pushed up from the ground and straggled away to merge into the outer darkness by their dog tents, until only two remained. One of these, tall, sharp-boned, angular, with the two worsted stripes of a corporal on the sleeve of his old blue coat, stretched at last to his feet and with one heavy shoe pushed the embers of the fire into it smaller glowing heap. He nudged the other with the toe of the shoe. "What ye waitin' for? The cap'n to come tuck ye in?" With a grunt the other heaved to his feet and the two moved away.

Quietly Captain Heath picked his way back to his tent. With the toe of one boot he too pushed the embers of the fire there into a smaller heap. He passed through the tent flaps and with the sureness of familiarity in the inner blackness felt for what he wanted. He emerged carrying a squat canvas stool and set this beside the little heap of embers. Relaxing to it, shoulders bent forward, he stared into the dwindling glow.

Overhead the wind freshened, fingering through the tops of the stunted pines. His head rose upright, alert. Floating on the wind from off to the west where the Orange Turnpike snaked through the Wilderness, came the muffled thud of hoofs. A single horse, traveling fast. The sound swelled and slid on past and faded toward corps headquarters near the old tavern.

Silence again except for the soft rustling overhead, and still he sat upright, straining for sound. It was there and not there and then again there, first felt then imperceptibly rising to the thin edge of hearing, caught and lost and caught again and held, a far featureless rumbling that trembled along the feathered wings of the wind.

Captain Heath sat still, listening. He did not turn his head when Lieutenant Beatty, coatless, sock-footed, boots in one hand, hurried out of the darkness toward him.

"Do you hear it, sir?"

"Yes."

"They must be moving. In full force. Only artillery and supply wagons could carry all the way here."

Captain Heath stirred on his stool. "Certainly they're moving.

"But oughtn't we report it, sir?"

Again that edge of irritation, sharpening the tone. "Use your head a bit, Beatty. We have pickets well out the turnpike. They've already sent word."

Lieutenant Beatty seemed to shrink smaller in the darkness, some of the eagerness seeping out of him. He shifted his weight from one socked foot to the other. "What do you think it means, sir?"

"How the devil would I know?" Captain Heath was startled at his own sudden vehemence. He spoke again with deliberate patience. "If it means what we want it to mean, they're moving south too. They'll be swinging over to intercept us in the open country below this confounded forest. I take it that's what Grant wants."

Lieutenant Beatty chewed this in quiet thought. He shifted the boots to his other hand and stared down at the silent figure of Captain Heath.

"But—but, Captain—"

"Yes?"

"Well . . . You can't ever be sure what General Lee will do. Can you, sir?"

"No," said Captain Heath. He raised one hand and pushed his campaign cap up and rubbed across his forehead where the band had pressed. "No. You can't." His hand dropped and he was motionless again on his stool.

Lieutenant Beatty peered into the thick clogged darkness as if by a sheer effort of will he could penetrate into the distance. He shifted his weight back to the other foot. He cleared his throat, a small nervous sound.

"For God's sake, Beatty!" Captain Heath was half turned, throwing the low intense words directly at him. "We're into this now. Nothing you do or I do tonight can change a thing. Get some rest."

Hesitant, hit, Lieutenant Beatty stepped back. He turned and slipped softly away, leaving Captain Jared Heath alone by the last embers of his fire, looking westward into the blank darkness, listening to a far faint throbbing of indistinguishable distant sounds in the night.

Morning, early, and in the half-light of dawn they shook out of bivouac and assembled along the road and in the scant open spaces near Wilderness Tavern. Clear and cool the light increased, showing the fresh new spring leaves along the bush branches and the violets in the grasses where no heavy shoes had yet trod, and even in this tangled Wilderness there was still some of the pageantry and high thrilling uplift of the storied war of storybooks and homefire tales with uniforms still neat and colorful and regimental flags flying and the bugles calling one to another and the drums rolling down the column as if fed forward into motion.

The main body of this wide column started on southward. A single division was ordered off westward on the Orange Turnpike to watch the flank and the 12th Massachusetts with it. The sun rose behind these men marching westward on the turnpike, filtering its light through the trees where these thinned close to the roadway, and briefly there was a renewed brightness with them and the night stiffness left their legs. The uneasiness of the dark hours dwindled as the minutes passed and they moved westward and there was nothing but the white dusty road and the hushed Wilderness hemming close on either side and their own skirmish line up ahead feeling the way forward. They moved westward and the minutes passed and their skirmish line dipped out of sight ahead where the ground dropped beyond a long rise and there was only the silent shadowy growth-clogged land and the road snaking gray-white and empty through it.

Captain Jared Heath, leading his company in steady stride, had a momentary impression that the war itself was unreal, something far off and remote and only imagined, and the single reality was the clean freshness of this spring morning in northern Virginia. Abruptly it passed and with a feeling of inevitability, of confirmation of foreboding, he halted as the ranks ahead of him were halting.

There was no signal, only an instinctive sharing of shock, and the whole first brigade stopped, the cessation of forward momentum beginning up front where the brigadier and his staff led in a mounted group and continuing back along the line. Dust swirled in the roadway ahead as a courier from the skirmishers on out of sight pulled his horse to it sliding stop to report. A convulsive ripple ran back along the column, men turning to send the word in low-voiced tense jerkiness: *Rebels! Coming this way!*

The brigadier snapped his orders and his aides scattered to carry them back along the column. Battle formation, astride the road and fanning out into the Wilderness on either side.

Captain Jared Heath, turning to take his men off to the left, felt the warmth of sun on his cheek and caught the fleeting scent of honeysuckle and remembered spring in Massachusetts and the fencerow lilacs and now it was all that which seemed unreal and remote and forsaken. He turned his back on the brief brightness of the roadway and led his company of hard-core regulars into the shadowed gloom of the Wilderness.

Fifty feet in and the dark woodland closed about them, shutting off all view of movement only a short distance away. The road itself, the link leading back to the main body of the army, was gone, lost, as if it no longer even existed. No parade ground maneuvers here. Impossible to form a proper battle line with the thickets and heavy underbrush bending and breaking it. Tall thin saplings that stretched upward searching for light waved and whipped into men's faces and the dry stuff and tangled vines underfoot clutched at ankles and tripped the unwary.

The line formed, ragged and rough, four-ranks deep, and behind it another in support, and they started forward and from on ahead came the first scattered shots as the skirmishers opened fire. They forced their way forward, the immediate enemy the Wilderness itself, and the first wisped taint of gunsmoke trailed to them under the low branches and they came abreast of the skirmish line. Ahead was only more of the Wilderness, dim, impenetrable to sight, already clouding with acrid smoke, and out of the dimness came increasing fire, in volleys now, from unseen opposing ranks, and they drove forward, steady under orders straight and unaware as yet into the center of a strong rebel assault force, stopping to fire and dropping to reload, ripping the cartridges open with their teeth and ramming the charges home, and rising in half-crouch to drive forward and fire again . . .

That was the beginning. As word went back to the temporary headquarters by Wilderness Tavern and the sound of firing climbed and carried back too, Grant understood at last that Lee had done it again, to him as to others before him, had refused to be drawn where wanted, had picked his own battleground where the heavy numerical superiority of the Union troops would be least effective and was forcing a full-scale battle there in the dark woodland. The massive Union movement southward stopped and drew in on itself and faced westward. Down on the Plank Road, two miles south of the turnpike, cavalry patrols collided with another rebel assault column and fighting flared there too and division after division plowed up to the battle lines spreading ever farther through the Wilderness. Artillery was all but useless here except in narrow enfilades down the roads themselves, and the high-pitched crackling roar of rifle fire dominated all else, swirled through the deepening smoke-clogged dimness at a pace and on a scale never before known and became a continuous, nerve-wrenching tumult and fires lit by the hot gun flashes crept through the underbrush and fallen timber and were whipped into leaping flames by a rising wind.

It has all long since been worked out with neat precision by historians, pinpointed on detailed maps, the two full days of hard-hammering slugging action, most of it back and forth over the same blood-drenched smoldering stretches of Wilderness waste-land, dwindling at last on the third day to a stalemate with the battered stripped armies about where they had been at the beginning and shading away that night into a race southward for possession of the vital crossroads at Spotsylvania Court House. It has been reduced, just another battle in a series of battles, to neatly proportioned paragraphs in history: the shifting positions of the various divisions and corps, the maneuvers attempted and made, the casualties climbing to one hundred deaths a minute and holding there hour after hour, the quiet determination of Grant steadily ordering troops forward, taking every setback as simply a signal to throw more men into the fight, the intuitive tactical genius of Lee shining clear even in that murky blind-bound Wilderness as he felt for and found soft spots in the Union lines and struck slashing into them.

You can follow the battle on the maps and in the accounts

written in the serene perspective of hindsight piecing together a coherent whole out of the scattered data assembled in the long aftermath. This you can say, pegging it all in concise phrases, is how it began, how it developed, the pattern it followed, the results attained.

To the men themselves who wrenched that data out of the bitterest fighting of a long bitter war, the men caught in the whip-lash of front-line action, there was no pattern, no real sense of taking part in coordinated battle movements. There was only a vast confused stumbling jumble of seemingly isolated fierce encounters between small broken units unable to keep contact with their fellows, unable to see more than a few yards ahead or around, an eerie groping struggle against an enemy seen only in spurts of gun flame out of smoke-shrouded thickets and ravines or suddenly met head on, face-to-face, in direct bodily grapple. Whole divisions were broken and dispersed, regiments scattered into small groups clinging together. Again and again men could not know whether the gunfire blazing on their flanks came from friends or foes, could not even determine the direction of the deadly shot decimating them. And cutting through the forest gloom, and the smoke-fog trapped under the trees, more terrify-ing in message of lurking unseen horror than the directionless pulsing roar of guns all around and the seeming lost isolation in the midst of furious unfathomed tumult, came the stench of burning flesh as the creeping fires claimed the dead and the still-living wounded as well.

Jared Heath fought through that battle, all of it, he and his battered, dwindling company. Through the long first day in the continuous driving disordered fighting along the turnpike that saw the Union forces smashed back almost to Wilderness Tavern and Grant's temporary headquarters threatened. Through the longer second day in the tremendous massed Union attack along the Plank Road, which in turn was twisted and torn and flung back in a flaming holocaust that halted only when full darkness cloaked the field. Through the third dragging day of stalemate and small clashes of patrols that probed the charred Wilderness as the two armies, exhausted and crippled, reluctant to renew the fight, sought to detect each other's movements and intentions. And that night, the night of the third day, he was in the forefront of the hurried march southward, the race toward Spotsylvania Court House that would be his last march, not his last march in uniform, but his last with the Army of the Potomac.

He fought through it all and as the regimental records and the company report book indicate, right up to the day—the fourth day—his name was stricken from the roster, he must have fought in all outward action at least resolutely and well. His company never broke apart, never faltered, never gave ground except under orders. Certainly that steadiness, grained in his men, must have come in part from the man himself. And yet, when he sought to reconstruct in his own mind the rushing eternity of this battle, not so much this battle as his own part in it, first in the urgency of the following days and again with that strange impersonal detachment of the later years, he could recall very little of the actual fighting. It had for him, as for so many others who endured the full brunt of its boiling confusion, the vague shimmering unreality of a nightmare with no orderly sequence of events, no sense of time moving measured ahead. Whole hours were gone, erased from memory not by any conscious or unconscious effort of will but probably by the sheer repetitious monotony of the very fierceness of the action in which the same things seemed to be happening and rehappening to no foreseeable purpose and with no discernible result except the staggered bloody dwindling of his company. At such times he must have carried on instinctively, the whole war, this battle, the whole past and present and future and the immensity of the wide world narrowed down to a shifting patch of all but impassable, death-drenched, dark woodland and the instant immediate unremitting effort to hold his men together and maintain contact with the rest of the regiment.

Individual moments alone could be regained and these too were winnowed in his mind's long search for significance until only a few remained. Surely these, if there is anything regainable now, offer some hint of the inward path the man was following. They have no weight in military judgment, which clings to a single act at issue as complete in itself, in his case held to a single word spoken on the morning of the fourth day on the rim of the little valley rolling down to the Spotsylvania road; but surely they bear some weight in the balance of any judgment, at least any understanding, of the man himself, the solitary unique segment of mortality for whom that act, that word spoken, could be only one point, however important, in the long-drawn journey of life.

This was the morning of the first day, in the tangled wasteland along the turnpike, when the hard fact was being hammered out that they had collided, not with any thin skirmish line or flank guard, but with the main body of Lee's veterans moving up to attack.

They had gone to earth like moles, dropping below the raking rebel fire that swept like a giant scythe slicing saplings and bush branches a few feet above the ground, belly-flat behind fallen timber or in small, hasty bayonet-scooped hollows where thickets gave close cover. The shock of their own advance had sent the first rebel line staggering back, and the second, and driving forward into increasing steadying resistance they had struck against the rebel reserves. Now they were clinging to their own position, anchor company at the left end of their own jagged regimental line that was lost to them in all but sound of firing off to their right. From far down the gloomed clogged aisles of the woodland, from their own immediate left and from beyond the rest of their regiment to the right, they could hear the reverberating, crackling roar of battle spreading ever farther out on the wings.

Colonel Goddard, ranging just behind his section of the line, face flushed and eyes red-rimmed from the smoke, scenting perhaps in the heavy tainted air his long sought brigadier's star, had stumbled out of the murk to peer along their hastily improvised entrenchments and nod approval. "Hang on here! The whole corps'll be coming up!" He had disappeared again off to the right, a stalwart soldierly shape suddenly there and as suddenly gone, and they maintained their wall of fire against the opposing fire that rose in intensity and came closer and slackened and fell back and once for a few seconds as a wind out of nowhere whipped aside the smoke clouds they saw a few gray-clad figures dodging into the dimness and fading again with only the flame-spurting Wilderness confronting them. Time burned upward into a strange timelessness and no reinforcements came from the rest of the corps floundering lost and forgotten somewhere behind them in the enveloping woodland, and the smoke thickened and clung heavily over all, and abruptly Captain Jared Heath was aware of himself, sword in hand, throat raw from unremembered orders shouted against the beating tumult, crouched behind a rotted stump, staring off to the left.

The battle sounds there had changed, shifted, seemed to be moving back, swinging in an arc and pressing closer. Faint but clear, sliding through the rattle of rifle fire, from behind the line of their own position, he heard the high keening scream of the rebel yell, derisive and triumphant, and the worst fear of the front line, intensified by the invisibility of the menace, raced shaking through him. Flanked! Rigid, unable to move, he stared toward the left. Out of the blankness, blurred and indistinct, plunged a blue-clad figure, running headlong, angling toward the rear. It tripped and fell and the rifle clutched in its hands flew aside and it scrambled up, heedless of the gun, and plunged frantic in flight on into the blankness behind, and as abruptly as before Captain Jared Heath was aware of his own men, those he could make out close at hand, looking at him.

They had ceased fire and the rush of battle elsewhere in the Wilderness dropped out of existence and in this dark pocket of silence their grimed, powder-blackened faces were turned toward him and the terrible tearing responsibility of command was a weight holding him helpless. Renewed volleys driving closer crashed out of the clouded woods just ahead of them. The feel, the very smell, of panic was there, grasping to take them, and they held firm, silently fighting it, looking at him, waiting. A flame of pride in them like a pain flashed through him and with it a sense of unutterable loss that the old man, the first Jared Heath, was not there to see them. A hoarse whisper that he thought was a shout scratched his throat. "Steady! Resume fire!" Somehow they caught it, perhaps not the words, perhaps only the sight of him jerking around to face forward again, shifting his sword to his left hand and taking his pistol in the right, and their own fire, spotty and increasing, built up again along the company front. Scattered shots were breaking in now from the left and sharp and distinct the thought hit him. The whole damned rest of the army's gone, we'll hold our own flank, and he peered through the dimness for Lieutenant Beatty to pull in his platoon back along the left and whirled, startled, at the sound of his own name.

"Heath!" Major Moody, out of nowhere, out of the lost cloaked confusion of the forgotten elsewhere of the fighting, limped hurrying toward him, dropping to half crouch beside him. "Good God, man! Didn't the message get through? The whole line's cracking! Back, man, back! On the double! We'll dig in with the corps if we can find the blasted snails!"

Only that, with clarity and completeness, out of the whole first day, out of all the daylight hours alternately dragging or swiftly telescoped in the turmoil of retreat and confused hurried regrouping and renewed advance crumpled again and thrown back and stiffening into murderous rifle-duel fighting from ground cover and improvised breastworks that died away slowly and stubbornly only in the temporary finality of full darkness.

Only that, and a few seconds snatched like a camera snapshot out of the afternoon, a picture distinct in every detail of himself down on one knee holding in one hand the tiny torn lifeless body of a small bird. He was shocked, shaking with the realization that for uncounted hours he had been seeing death with unseeing eyes, blinded by the callous necessitous indifference of battle tension, stumbling upon with no real awareness and striding over or around the bodies of men lying limp and lifeless in a battle-wracked dark woodland. He felt his lips curl in unwilled ironic bitterness at the thought it had taken a few bloody feathers he could cradle in one cupped hand, a single insignificant small token of destruction, accidental, purposeless, to bring this into focus for him. For an instant he saw himself alien to everything about him, out of place, out of time, and he flinched inward away from the death that smirched the air everywhere and searched in its own callous indifference for targets out of the hidden places and he rocked with the unwilled sweeping urge to be out of it, away from it, free from it, abstracted clean and young and untainted out of the whole of known existence.

An instant only, etched forever into his mind, and again, now by a conscious effort of will, he was Captain Jared Heath, third of the name to follow the old flag, taking the thinned ranks of his company forward across fought-over charred wasteland . . .

Night. The two armies had not drawn apart, simply sprawled as darkness had found them in splintered formations through the Wilderness. The narrow space between the jagged lines was a fearful forbidden territory where slow fires smoldered in the underbrush and nervous advanced pickets blazed at any unidentified sound or movement and the cries of wounded, lost and unclaimed in the dark thickets, drifted desperately on the shifting night winds. In the black reaches behind the front, unending activity wore away the sleepless hours as officers strove to sort out scattered regiments and brigades and stragglers wandered in search of their units and deserters crept off in the cloaking dark and orders direct from staff headquarters sent hurriedly assembled columns struggling through the confusion into position for what the morning would bring.

He sat on a short upturned piece of log, back against the trunk of a stunted pine. The canvas of an old dog tent, pegged to the ground and fastened to a branch above, kept the wind from a candle on another piece of log close to his right leg. The scant flickering light fell on the company roster book spread open on his knees. There had been eighty-two names on the active list that morning, officers and men, a sound, full battle-campaign company. There were fifty-nine now. Down the pages neatly labeled "Dead and Wounded" ran new lists in his firm slanting script. On the page labeled "Deserters" stood one name.

No need to sit there studying a thin, cardboard-covered

army-issue book marred by pencil markings in his own hand. His report had gone to Colonel Goddard and on to corps headquarters. The weary march southward into place for the new morning's renewed assault out along the Plank Road was over. Now was the time to snatch what rest was possible in the last hours before dawn. And still he sat motionless, staring at the open pages on his knees.

How long he sat there he could not know. Time was nothing, an empty blankness. He looked up. A dark shape stood before him, tall, lank, angular. In the feeble glimmer of the candle reaching out he could barely distinguish the long, gaunt, thorn-scratched face under an almost shapeless forage cap and the two dirtied stripes of a corporal on the torn sleeve of the old blue coat.

"Hagan's come in, Cap'n."

He straightened on the piece of log, alert, aware in the living passing moment. "What does he say?"

"Says he got mixed with some Vermonters goin' back and couldn't find us after. . . You want I should bring him over?"

"Do you believe him?"

"Hagan's all right, Cap'n. Kept lookin'. Found us. All the way we come to here."

Silence. He looked down at the open page with the one name written on it. He took a small, slate pencil from a pocket and drew a line through the name. He stared down at it and with careful strokes drew more lines through it and rubbed the pencil point back and forth over it, marking it out, unreadable.

"They sure give us hell today, didn't they, Cap'n?"

He looked up again. The tall shape, lank and angular, stretching up into the first branches of the low pine, was still there, looking down at him and the open book on his knees.

"What'll be in the mornin', Cap'n? We try an' give it back agin?"

He could feel, sense, grasp without hearing the mute unbreathed appeal in the voice reaching past regulations and all the rigid suddenly valueless barriers between for some contact, some assurance, some touch of sharing in the battle-scarred blackness of this night. He sought to speak and could not, the muscles of his throat tight and aching, and the tall shape spoke again. "Sorry, Cap'n. Reckon I talked out of turn." It moved away, receding into the darkness, and he felt an overwhelming helpless, futile desire to leap after it, to hold it, to make it understand, and as if the very intensity of his desire had leaped for him he sensed rather than saw it hesitate and half turn and the voice came gently to him. "Don't be frettin' any, Cap'n. We'll be there with you, tryin'."

He heard a small cracking sound and a pain stabbed through his right hand. He looked down. The slate pencil had snapped and one of the jagged ends of the break was dug deep into the flesh of his hand.

It was their turn again in this deadly game shuttling confused and directionless through fought-over ravaged wilderness. They were driving ahead again now and they broke into a small clearing, weed-grown, dry, and crackling underfoot, and they saw gray-clad figures running for the woods on the other side and some falling under their fire and they drove forward in pursuit, into the open, out across the clearing, straight into sudden sweeping volleys that crashed out of the thickets ahead. Broken, crumpled, they stopped as if they had struck against a solid invisible wall. Those who could turned and ran back, diving headlong into cover, and the fighting here in this isolated sector of the long boiling battle front settled again to a rifle duel across a small dry weedy clearing strewn now with the bodies of dead and wounded.

He was aware of himself, flat along needled ground, peering through matted growth out over the clearing, his mind working desperately on some problem. Then full awareness washed over him. He was striving to determine how many blue-clad bodies blotted the open space, lying limp and motionless or struggling in frantic jerky movement toward the protection of the dark woods. And then that problem was gone, whipped away by the cold paralyzing realization of the hidden horror of this battle, cloaked elsewhere by the rank growth and vine-clogged trees and the smoke-shroud trapped under the branches, stripped here open and raw to sight at last. Out of the woods to the left where thick smoke clouds rolled through the trees little flames licked at the edge of the clearing. Caught by wind they snatched at the dry, low, weedy growth and flared up racing reaching into the open. They closed around the hatless head and the shoulders of a blue-clad body and blazed brighter in its hair and leaped to reach the cartridge box at the waist and the thudding crackle of the explosions shook the limp body and shredded cloth and flesh along the side. They reached on, spreading, remorseless, and caught the near side of a taller patch of dry last-season growth and climbed clutching at it and inching out of the other side jerked a gray-clad figure grabbing at the ground with frantic fingers, dragging useless legs, and they leaped with the strength of fresh fuel to grasp the legs and flare forward feeding on gray cloth. The crippled figure thrashed on the ground and a high thin scream was torn from the tortured throat, intolerable, unending, strangled at last in a gasping, gurgling dwindle as the flames claimed the entire body and the muffled thudding of exploding cartridges ripped it twitching into stillness.

He rose upright, heedless of the brambles and branches raking his face as he came to his feet. He was conscious of a man near him to the right, bent over, retching violently, of the colorless horror-held face of Lieutenant Wilkeson somewhere in the bushes to the left, and these were unimportant details in the overall indelible picture of open sky, innocent and serene and lovely over a small clearing where little flames hunted eagerly for the living and the dead with impartial, indifferent hunger, and beyond was the dark edging of woodland where hidden rifles laced the thickets. His mind, recoiling from a searing, senseless affront to the very fact of existence, from the knowledge that he was in it, was a part of it, seemed sunk in an unbreakable weariness tinged with a kind of madness, a dim, distant hope that a bullet from one of the hidden rifles would find him.

There were no bullets from the hidden rifles. There was only the brooding clamor of battle elsewhere in the Wilderness and the terrible thudding explosions of cartridges in the clearing. And across from the opposite side, hoarse and angry and somehow clean and cleansing in its very hoarseness and anger, came a sound of sanity, a flash of invincible faith in the remote ineradicable war-throttled humanity of the race. "To hell with you Yanks! We're getting our men!" He saw gray-clad figures emerge from the opposite woods, running out to beat at the flames about the wounded and drag them back into the dimness, and abruptly he broke out of the weariness, flooded with strength, tireless, striding through the underbrush to drive men who needed no driving into the clearing to recover their own.

And moments later, when the clearing was lost in its smoke and that rolling in from the left and they were back in the woods and what could be done had been done and he knew with an unreasoned simple certainty that the rebel assault would come angling around the smoke-held clearing from the right and had his remaining men ready for it, he found himself waiting, listening, without knowing exactly for what, and it came, out of the veiled woods to the right, hoarse and not angry, a voice never to be identified and never to be forgotten, fulfilling an ancient, gallant obligation that had no place in the insensate savagery of this battle, of this war and what it was becoming, and yet was miraculously and defiantly there. "All right, Yanks! We're coming at you!"

They were staggering back, stubbornly making it a retreat not a rout, fire and drop back and reload and fire again. Behind them, where the woodland thinned, they glimpsed the log breastworks they had left long hours before, strengthened more now, and behind that masses of blue-clad reserves taking position back of the logs, and they ran the last distance and scrambled over and to the relative safety beyond, out of the way of the reserves, and dropped exhausted to the ground.

He paced slowly past ragged men sprawled limp and weary, checking the familiar figures known instantly each through the grime and the blood and the sweat and the powder-black. Thirty-four. Worn, blunted, the movement of his mind requiring conscious effort, he began the count again and was interrupted by a raw, croaking shout that cut through the battle tumult whirling back from the breastworks and that battered at his eardrums. "Beatty! Where's Beatty?" He stopped and his jaws clamped tight, clenched, rigid in the realization that the voice was his own.

Night again. The two armies had drawn back in the darkness, held apart now by the very destruction they had wrought, by stretches of wracked wilderness where lingering flames and choking smoke checked all movement and of charred, horror-soaked ground where bivouac was impossible. There was no pressure of the enemy close, ominous in presence only earshot away, of picket clashes just outside campfire light that might develop into stabbing raids. Sleep should have been possible this night and was not, except in fitful, drugged snatches of complete exhaustion that left untouched the bone-deep weariness within.

He lay on a blanket, half reclining against the inside bottom slope of an earth-and-log barricade. He lay quiet, unthinking, and heard without hearing the low distant rumble of wagon trains of wounded moving northward in the night. Overhead, through a rift in the clouds that worked up out of the Wilderness and drifted with the wind, he saw without seeing the deep blue-black of open sky and the remote lonely pinpointed flicker of a few stars.

"This way, sir." The voice of Lieutenant Wilkeson penetrated to him from somewhere beyond where his men lay in their own tired sleeplessness by the last of several small campfires. "Over here, sir."

He sat up and made out the dim shape of Wilkeson moving toward him and beside it the tall unmistakable outline of Colonel Goddard. He pushed to his feet, fighting through weariness to come to attention.

"At ease, Heath." Colonel Goddard turned slightly toward the figure beside him. "Thank you, Lieutenant. That will be all."

Curious, reluctant, Lieutenant Wilkeson moved away and Colonel Goddard stepped to the barricade and turned to lean back against it. "Snap out of it, man. There's nothing official in this."

He was suddenly aware that he was still standing stiff, erect, and he relaxed and moved slowly to join the other against the barricade. He leaned against it, silent, waiting.

Colonel Goddard sighed, betraying his own weariness beneath

the hard, habitual, old-army shell of indomitable competence. "I said this wasn't official, Heath, and it isn't, not yet, but I thought I'd tell you. We'll be getting replacements in a few days. God knows we need them. After what's happened the whole regiment will have to be reorganized. I'm thinking of putting your men in with Captain Clemmons's company."

"No!" He was startled at the swiftness, at the vehemence, of his own instinctive unthinking response.

"Eh?" Colonel Goddard peered at him in the darkness. "Don't want to lose your company? Is that it? Why, man, I'm thinking of you too. That will free you for another assignment. Staff work. Probably at brigade headquarters. Why, man, watch your step and your chances and there's no better spot for promotions."

"No!" His mind, prodded into alertness, grappled with vague, unformulated feelings beyond grasp. He was conscious of the other's affront, withdrawal, of a gulf between, unbridgeable, and the necessity of speaking, of communicating, bore upon him. Even as he spoke he knew the words were pitiful, inadequate. "I guess I don't want the outfit to go out of existence, sir."

"I see." Colonel Goddard spoke slowly and the fact that he did not see and could not see was an almost palpable presence between them. "We are fighting a war, Heath, and what any one man wants is not important. Except to himself. When you've been in the army as long as I have, you'll understand that."

There was no answer, none that would convey meaning, and they leaned against the barricade, each in his own immovable isolation, and a voice carried faintly to them. "Christ almighty! I can't sleep! Ain't there anyone can even raise a tune?"

Silence, except for the far rumbling of heavy wagon wheels. Then another voice, raucous even at the distance, from a smoke-raw throat:

Oh I wish I was in the land of cotton,
Old times there—

"Not that, ye goddamned jackass!"

Silence again. And into the silence, creeping, feeling for the words and lifting melancholy melody, another voice, hoarse and haunting:

I know moon-rise,
I know star-rise,
Lay this body down . . .

It rose, surer, more certain, floating slow and soft on the wind,

I walk in the moonlight,
I walk in the starlight . . .

and another voice with it now, softly building the refrain,

Lay this body down . . .

and more voices, restrained, holding back for the one, rising with the refrain:

I'll walk in the graveyard,
I'll walk through the graveyard,
To lay this body down
I go to the judgment in the evening of the day
When I lay this body down . . .

Abruptly Colonel Goddard pushed out from the barricade. "Good men, Heath. Damned good men. There's an old army saying, as long as men can sing they can fight."

It came rushing from him, unaware, intense. "And how many of them will be alive to sing tomorrow night? Or the night after?"

The tall figure beside him straightened, stiffened, in the single slight movement somehow raising again the fact of rank between them. "All of them, I hope, Captain. But take my advice and stay away from such thoughts. That is what men are put into uniform for, to obey orders and to fight and if necessary to die . . ."

He was alone, leaning back against the barricade, arms outstretched on either side, hands gripping the top log. Dim, distant, incredibly remote, words carried to him. "You finished, Hank? I thought they was more."

Silent, aching, he listened, straining motionless toward the sound that must come, whose not coming would leave him forever lost and straining toward it, and it came, slow and low, whispering along the wind:

And my soul and your soul will meet in the day
When I lay this body down . . .

Out of the whole third day, nothing retained, nothing clear and with continuity, only a remembered sense of waiting, of endless activity and yet of waiting, of endless trivial post-battle activity welcome as it occupied the minutes and the mind, and yet through it, over it, dominating it, of waiting. A day of plodding patrol duty, of checking equipment, of recounting losses, of bringing in the last of the reclaimable wounded. And of waiting.

The entire army was waiting. It knew it had been met and matched, its superior, outnumbering weight blocked and broken and thrown back. As the hours wore on and the patrols scouting the burnt-over, ruined Wilderness encountered no rebel advance, no more than occasional skirmishers on the same obvious errand, it knew that this battle, this phase at least of this battle, was over. And all this had happened before, not with the same brutal bloody bitterness, but with the same inescapable realization of having been blocked, broken, thrown back. And always before, in the orders from headquarters, had come acceptance of defeat, withdrawal northward to reorganize and reequip and absorb new recruits and rebuild strength for some new commander's new plan. The unknown, the imponderable now, was that stubby, stubborn, little man named Grant. And the waiting held, all through the day, even into the first hours of the night when orders finally came stepping down the chains of command and the army pulled out of its trenches, from behind its barricades, and assembled weary and still waiting in marching columns—and found itself moving, not northward toward rest and furloughs and settled camp routine, but southward toward the certainty of renewed hammering, bitter battle.

That was the turning point for the Army of the Potomac; the time that can be cited almost to the exact hour, when it knew that it had its man at last and that it could be licked and licked again and never again defeated, and tired and grim and stumbling in the dark it faced southward toward eventual victory.

Was that too the turning point for Captain Jared Heath? Was his sense of waiting more than that which gripped the army as a whole, not simply a wondering what would happen next but an obscure knowing, not acknowledged perhaps even to himself, that he had changed, altered inalienably now, and that somewhere sometime ahead circumstance would overwhelm him? There is no certain answer. All that can be regained of those days in the Wilderness, of his days in the Wilderness, has been told. He was marching now, southward with the 12th Massachusetts down the Brock Road through the lower edge of the Wilderness, perhaps already committed to it, toward his own individual destiny . . .

There had been cheers, scattered along the columns, from worn-raw throats, and briefly the men had shaken off weariness when they reached the road and swung south and the meaning sank into them. Now they were silent, plodding in the deep road dust, stumbling into one another, dragging strength for each forward step out of the depths of near exhaustion, men who had been through two days of almost continuous fighting and another of tense waiting with scant sleep and no real rest. Here and there men staggered and fell, crawling to collapse by the roadside, and the file closers, following close behind each unit, had a dreary task to do. The urgency working down from the officers driving them communicated to them and died away and rose again under effort and died away again in slow succeeding waves into the weary plodding. Far ahead was the vital crossroads at Spotsylvania Court House. If they could reach it, fortify it, they would have the initiative, the position, threatening Lee's long flank toward Richmond, and he would be compelled to wear away his lesser forces battering against them. That was a hope, a purpose, glimmering far ahead. Here and now was the endless implacable necessity of dragging forward in the dark through dust that rose unceasing and sifted over and into all.

Forward and halt, while somewhere ahead men swung axes to clear the narrow road of logs lopped down and across by wide-ranging rebel cavalry, and forward again, sodden-limbed, dropping into fitful dozing as if drunk even while still upright, moving, and catching awake and staggering on.

The first wan light of dawn and they were moving through more open country, farmland now, rolling, cut into fields, and ahead some of their own cavalry was running into resistance, rebel skirmishers behind fencerows and brush piles. The crackle of carbine fire came sharp and distinct and they fanned out, stumbling with weariness, in makeshift battle formation, out across the fields, and pushed ahead, scattering the thin, merely delaying rebel line, and on into a narrow stretch of woods rimming a long, low ridge and emerged on the other side and stopped, held, halted by sheer exhaustion and the scene before them.

Clean and green and lovely in the growing light the ground fell away into a small valley, sloped down to the road that ran on to Spotsylvania Court House and rose again to another wooded ridge that dominated, commanded, the sweep of valley and the road below. And along that opposite ridge, plainly seen among the trees, gray-clad figures, many, too many, were digging trenches and raising hasty breastworks of fence rails and dirt.

Captain Jared Heath, standing spraddle-legged to remain erect, his mind curiously detached from his tired sagging body, saw the whole scene of which he was a single small part, the whole enveloping situation, with a cold logical clarity. Here, on this side, one brigade, the strung-out ragged remainder of one brigade, worn almost past endurance, with the rest of the division, of the corps, of the whole army, spread out in long marching columns miles behind and away on narrow traffic-jammed roads, and across on the other side, strong and perhaps impregnable in already partially fortified position, an unknown number of rebels increasing as more of them filed into view through the trees. He felt a flicker of admiration, impersonal, untouched by any emotion, for that great legendary man in gray, commander and symbol and soul of the enemy army, who had again, in time, foreseen, forestalled, and that passed, forgotten, as the thought hit him of struggling leaden-limbed up that opposite slope into raking rebel fire; and he shuddered, recoiling from it, and a wave of relief washed through him as the simple, sane, inevitable logic of the situation unrolled before him. They were checked, blocked, in no position or strength to strike further. There was nothing to be done but to hold where they were, to seize what rest was possible, until the whole corps came up and artillery with it and the enemy stand could be assessed and tested and a battle plan evolved.

He saw the brigadier and the division commander and staff officers with them ride forward to the edge of the slope off to the, left and look out over the valley and the corps commander himself come pounding forward to join them. He saw them talking together and he knew, calm, convinced in the certainty of his own inescapable logic, what they were saying. He looked away again at the opposite ridge, studying the activity there. To the right where the ridge swung inward, flanking the immediate slope rising to the hasty fortifications, a few gray-clad figures could be seen, scouting the position there, and that fact too clicked into place in his mind.

He saw the staff officers now ranging out along the ragged line of which he was a part and one of them leaning down from the saddle to speak to Colonel Goddard and then the colonel coming toward him and he straightened, waiting, a good soldier, a competent battle-tested officer of the line waiting for the orders already framed, complete, intact, in his own mind—and these fell rushing into the abyss of a darkness without meaning under the impact of the colonel's eager red-flecked eyes in the stern dusk-mask of a face.

"Get your men ready, Heath. This is our chance to grab hold of glory. We're going to drive them out of there."

He rocked without moving, rigid, imprisoned in the relentless instant. Again the thought hammered at him, detailed, fully realized, of struggling up, of leading his men, up the opposite slope, up into the death trap waiting for them, and he collapsed inward away from it and a desperation drove him stumbling to grasp at the arm of Colonel Goddard moving, hurrying on. "My God, sir! It's impossible! Inhuman! The men can hardly stand!"

Colonel Goddard stopped, half turned, impatient, on the edge of anger. "The enemy are just as tired, man. We'll hit them before they can bring up any artillery."

"But there isn't a chance! Can't you see? Not a chance! Even fresh troops couldn't do it!"

Colonel Goddard turned more, facing him, full-front, anger breaking in his eyes. "Am I to understand, sir, that you refuse to lead your men into action?"

It came unsought, unsearched for, unbuttressed by any conscious reasoning, with a feeling of simple inevitability, out of whatever was unique, single, individual in the small isolated segment of mortality that was Jared Heath.

"Yes!"

From back in the shadow of the trees rimming the ridge he watched the battle line move forward, slow, too slow, weighted with weariness, down the near slope and across the valley floor, and start up the opposite slope. For a time he could make out his company, his no longer, Lieutenant Wilkeson in command, then they were lost, indistinguishable in distance and the terrible torn confusion along the still advancing front as the rebel fire from above swept it, volley after volley, searching, deadly, and what had been a battle line was no more than a staggering fringe of clotted groups of blue-clad men struggling upward. Then this thinned, leaving a track of dead and wounded behind it, and struggled on and halted, what remained, huddled low in the shelter of a small bank jutting out along the slope side. From the woods on the right where the ridge swung flanking inward, ranks of gray-clad men emerged and pushed out and dropped into position to send new fire sweeping across the slope into the huddled groups below the bank and the men there, unsheltered now, goaded, drove upward again in a last dragging attempt at a charge and faltered and turned and ran in flight, falling, stumbling, crawling, in the dreadful slow-motion desperation of complete, exhausted collapse.

He turned away, emptied of emotion, and started back through the trees. He moved slowly, unaware of the lagging, slow lurch of each slow step, holding at bay a nameless overwhelming loneliness only by the sheer deliberate effort of concentration on carrying out the one order it did not occur to him, could not occur to him, to disobey. "You are under arrest, sir. You will report back to the quartermaster and wait until I send for you."

Two

That fight too, pathetic, tragic, blundering, across that valley and up that slope into a section of what would be known in later fighting as the Bloody Angle, can be followed in the history books, some of them, tucked away in a paragraph or two. The brigade was smashed, ripped beyond recognition, and with it the rest of the division that came up and tried to advance in support and was caught in the same flanking crossfire as the rebel lines strengthened and spread. Not enough was left of the division to be worth reorganization. A few days later the fragments were assigned to other units. And that was only an incident in the almost constant battering butchery the war was becoming, beginning in the Wilderness and renewing overnight by the approaches to Spotsylvania Court House. The battle there widened as before in the Wilderness as more troops came up and the opposing lines lengthened ever farther out on the wings, and it settled into long days of assault and repulse and the death lists climbed inexorably and long trains of wounded rumbled without ceasing northeast toward Fredericksburg.

Jared Heath was out of it now, out of this battle and those that would follow, bound in his own personal battle with the consequences of his own irrecoverable act, of interest, in the perspective of the war, only as one of the drumhead court-martial cases marking the strange quirks of military justice in the heated backwash of the fighting itself. In the perspective of his own story, which is this story, he had not yet, not even yet, collided with the corrosive fact that would determine his destiny. And the key men here were two: one who should have known him and could not know him, Colonel Goddard, essentially a simple, uncomplicated man, unquestioningly old-army, who had seen his regiment ruined completely and his hopes of a brigadier's star blasted on a bloody hillside and was filled now, in the immediate aftermath, with cold, cankering, restrained, official fury; the other who had not known him before and knew him only briefly now and yet may have understood him better than he did himself, a Matthew Foster, a civilian lawyer brought into the War Department early in the war, serving now with rank of major as a judge advocate with the army in the field.

It was this Major Foster who saw him at the moment of collision and who, writing an account of the case for his personal files that would be the basis of his war reminiscences published years later, left a record of it.

The summons had come and he waited in the mid-afternoon sun, erect, outwardly calm, ready, and nearby a group of officers talked low-toned together by a wide plank laid across two small barrels and one of them separated and moved toward him, slim, slight, incredibly neat in uniform untouched by battle taint.

"Captain Heath?" The voice was cool, impersonal, official.

"Yes." He hesitated over the word that should follow and a thin, ironical smile hovered on the other's lips.

"Your instinct is sound, Captain. We can dispense with the

formalities. I am Major Foster. It is my duty, as judge advocate, to inform you that, as a commissioned officer, you may claim a general court-martial."

He was ready for this. "I want only one thing. To get it over with. As quickly as possible."

"Then you waive your claim and will submit to regimental proceedings?"

"Yes."

"Very well. It is also my duty, I regard it as such, to assist you in preparing your defense."

"Defense?" He was ready for this too. "There is none. None you can recognize." Then for a moment his reserve, his readiness, broke. "But I was right! Right! It was hopeless! Insane!" He quieted, withdrawn within himself. "That means nothing to the men who died because I was right. I refused to obey an order. I have no defense."

"But, Captain." The other's voice was still cool, impersonal, but no longer inflexibly official. "That is not the charge. The charge is cowardice. Cowardice in the face of the enemy."

Thunderstruck. The word is from Major Foster's personal notes.

The man was thunderstruck—firmly believe until that precise moment he had not understood what he had done—wrapped in himself—worked out some kind of rationalization—had not once thought what his action would mean to others—for a few seconds he was absolutely open—positively quivering—might say frightened—clear impression that afterwards through entire proceedings was hardly aware—almost indifferent—seemed to be puzzled—off somewhere in his own thoughts—time—time— never enough time on these things—would be interesting to know more of his background—

He did as he was told to do, mechanically, not really a part of this because it was nothing to him. The verdict, secret, sealed, had been hurried to corps headquarters and there approved, quickly, emphatically, as a pointed example at a time when desertions and lodgings of duty were becoming a serious problem. Now he waited without really waiting, doing what he was told to do.

He took the place assigned to him in front of, in plain view of the pitiful, withered remnant of the regiment assembled in scant close ranks along the edge of a wide field. Beyond the wooded ridge a half-mile away the roar of continuing spreading battle rumbled and reverberated with artillery in full action. Everywhere about was the hurrying confusing activity of troops moving up to the expanding front and supply wagons straining forward to advanced positions. Not here in this field where the brigade, what remained, had retired to regroup. Not here along this fencerow where the tired, tattered remnant of a regiment was assembled at the orders of its colonel.

And this was nothing to him, touched only the outer edge of his mind, unmeaning. He was alone with his own tormenting questing thoughts.

Out on the far rim of awareness Colonel Goddard had taken a stand near him, held a paper in his hand, was reading it aloud, and he forced a small, unimportant part of his mind to attention because that was expected of him.

Phrases only out of the wordy, involved maze of military legalism:

> . . . to be read aloud to the regiment . . . posted throughout the army . . . published in the journals of his home state . . . unmitigated cowardice . . . deliberate absence from duty when his men were tinder fire . . . to be stripped of all insignia . . . reduced to the

ranks . . . subject to further disciplinary action as deemed proper
by his commanding officer . . .

And still this was nothing to him, simply something happening removed, inevitable, to be endured, unimportant against the search—the question, that would be with him now forever. He stood erect, unflinching, as Colonel Goddard stepped close and reached and ripped the epaulettes with their two silver-embroidered bars from his shoulders, leaving jagged rents in the cloth of his coat, and stepped back, staring at him, baffled, fury rising, at his unflinching, enduring erectness.

"Buck this man!"

They tied his arms together at the wrists and pushed him to the ground, seated, and doubled his legs back tight together at the knees and pulled the tied arms down around them and forced a stick through, in the crook of the elbows, under the knees. Humped, helpless, jerked mercilessly into the immediate moment, he heard Colonel Goddard's voice, cold, furious, finding in simple, uncomplicated contempt the one approach that would rip him into final, raw, agonized awareness.

"This man has disgraced the regiment, all of us, every last one of us. We can repudiate it. And him. For my part I promise you that I shall have him transferred as soon as possible . . . By companies now, single file. You will march past him and each of you will spit upon him."

There were few of them, so pitifully few, and yet there was no end to the jarring impact of the passing figures, beating, unbearable, and the moist sticky stains on his clothes and boots, on the flesh of his face and tied hands, were acid marks sinking and merging to engulf his whole being. He sought after defiance and could not find it and held his eyes fixed low on the heavy, passing shoes unidentifiable in their anonymity and felt his mind, whirling, draw tighter and tighter in intolerable tension toward breaking and he sensed without knowing the line halting and pulled back his head to look up.

Tall, angular, the lank figure stretched above him, a breeze gently flapping the ragged, dirtied sleeve with its two worsted stripes of a corporal, the gaunt, grim, indomitable head sharp against the late afternoon sky. It stood quiet, motionless, looking down at him, and behind it other men, stopped, moved restlessly, and Colonel Goddard's voice came snapping, angry, and still it stood quiet, looking down.

The whirling in his mind ceased and the taut, intolerable tension remained and he knew with a sudden, terrible certainty that sanity would hold only under a fullness, a completeness, a finality, and his voice climbed, cracking, frenzied, urgent. "Yes! Yes! Do it! Damn you! Do it!"

He saw the head move slightly and he strained upward and caught the words that could save him. "All right, Cap'n." And the last word was a stabbing blessed pain and the man's spittle on his upraised face was almost a benediction. He dropped his head and was still, enduring.

A day, two days, a week? The exact lapse could perhaps be determined by a search, if they survive, of the corps quartermaster's records that must have carried the name of Private Jared Heath for the next brief period. But to what purpose any such search? Even if successful it could yield nothing of importance, of significance, simply the recorded fact that for a few days, transferred to the quartermaster's department, clad in the stiff, new-issue, dark blue jacket that was more a blouse and the light blue pants and heavy, black shoes and sloping-crown cap of a private, he served as assistant to the driver, officially known then as the conductor, of an ambulance wagon. What was important, if there was anything important during those few days until the last hours that ended them, was that he learned he was a marked man, branded as surely as with a hot iron, and this could be borne, almost welcomed except in sudden flashes of outcast pain, because it offered some obscure sense of expiation for the death of men who had died without him and because it paled against the steady, burning of the hidden questing question he could not answer.

The ambulance depot behind this sector of the long battle front was an old farmhouse with ramshackle outbuildings where medical officers, hollow-eyed, drunk with fatigue, fought their own losing battle to keep pace in emergency treatment with the unceasing stream of wounded and where orderlies picked their way, cursing their own tired clumsiness, over and around shattered, helpless figures that lay on obscenely dirtied blankets filling all available floor space.

He stood outside, ankle-deep in the dust of the dooryard, close-by the heads of a tired mule team hitched to a low, two-wheeled ambulance. It was emptied now. The last of the last trip's wounded had been carried inside where what could be done for them would be done and they would wait, those that lived, to be loaded again into the big vans of the wagon trains that rumbled irregularly northeastward toward the improvised hospitals at Fredericksburg.

He had swung the ambulance, leading the mules by the bridles, away from the platform that had been a porch, clearing the space for the next wagon already creaking into view under its dust cloud in the distance. In a moment his driver would reappear and they would start again on the routine that seemed to have had no beginning and would have no end, gathering and bringing back the broken, perhaps salvageable, human waste of warfare. The unremitting ache of long hours of physical labor was bedded deep in his muscles and he waited, quiet in a patience that was not a patience but a self-imposed endurance of the passage of time and a defense against existence.

Flies that fed on the clotted-blood drops in the dust, that bred in the thrown-aside offal of emergency operations, swarmed through the dooryard. The tired mules, twitching, stung, jerked against the traces and the ambulance moved slightly and a cloud of flies rose buzzing from the stained, sticky floorboards and settled again. The fact penetrated to him and he pulled his mind from its preoccupation with other things to consider it. He walked slowly around to the rear of the ambulance and scooped up handfuls of dust and threw these scattering in over the sticky stains. He looked about and saw an old, wooden rake, cracked and almost toothless, lying by the farmhouse wall. He took this and reached with the flat side down to rub the dust into the stains and scrape the boards clean again.

The driver appeared around a corner of the building and came toward the ambulance, passing him, ignoring him, and this was part of the routine, and he leaned the rake against the farmhouse wall and turned again to the ambulance and, forgetting, sank down, seated, on the lowered tailboard. At the sound of the voice, thick with weariness and habitual irritation and anger concentrated now on him, he remembered and pushed out and to his feet.

"I'll not be tellin' ya again, Heath. Next time I'll be usin' the whip. Ya'll walk. No yellowbelly rides my wagon."

This too was part of the routine, plodding behind the

ambulance in the wheel dust, along the route marked by red flags for the walking wounded to find their own way to the depot. Outward along the route, passing those walking, then swinging in behind the battle line to pick up those unable to walk, stretched waiting where comrades had laid them in some patch of shade, to load them like cordwood crammed side by side on the boards, cushioned where possible by rolled castaway coats and knapsacks, and back again along the route where the wheel ruts wore ever deeper into the rough ground.

They were coming back. Ahead, beside the rutted wheel tracks, a man walked, stumbled, staggered, right arm hanging limp, the sleeve and part of the jacket ripped away, upper arm and shoulder wrapped in improvised bloodstained bandage. The ambulance jolted closer, overtaking, and he stumbled on, weak, wobbling, and fell forward and down and tried to push up with left hand and arm and could not and rolled over on his back, staring up.

The ambulance stopped beside the still figure. Private Jared Heath moved out from his plodding position and around toward it. The driver, after one weary look at the overloaded wagon bed, hunched over to the outer edge of his seat and slapped the board beside him. "Get him up here."

He stood over the still figure and leaned down and in the act of leaning stopped, bent over, motionless, caught by the glare of the hot, feverish eyes staring up at him. The man's lips stirred in the powder-blackened face, twitched over the yellowish, tobacco-stained teeth. "Heath, ain't it?"

His mind leaped out of its lonely isolation, racing after recognition and there was none. The man was nameless to him, unknown, yet knew him, was a shattered casualty in need of his unblooded, unwounded strength. He dropped to one knee and reached to slip an arm under the man's left shoulder and in a sudden access of fury the man heaved bodily away on the ground and kicked at him.

"Don't touch me! Not a son-of-a-bitching coward like you!"

The stabbing pain of renewed, sharpened loneliness drove him to draw back. He saw the man, in the remaining impetus of rushing, indignant anger, stagger up and toward the ambulance and fall clutching at the near wheel with his left hand and claw forward to grasp the seat side and the driver lean to take hold of the arm and pull him sobbing in the agony of effort up to the seat.

The ambulance moved forward again, the tired mules heaving heavily into the traces. The driver held the reins in one hand and with the other supported the swaying figure close against him. And Jared Heath followed, walking alone in the wheel dust.

He led the tired mules, quivering, ready to drop, to the picket line behind the old barn and fastened them there beside others as tired. The few men about, moving away, avoiding him, were shadows outside any real awareness. He stripped off the harness and dragged this, trailing, into the lopsided lean-to that jutted out from the rear of the barn and hung it beside others on a spike driven into the wall.

"Heath?" There was no anger, no contempt in the voice, only a simple questioning. He turned in the dim interior and saw a man in the wrinkled, stained uniform of a hospital steward silhouetted against the lighted doorway. "You're Heath, aren't you?"

"Yes . . . I'm Heath."

And still there was no anger, no contempt in the voice, only a clean, passing, impersonal friendliness. "It's a hell of a way to run a war. This has been kicking around all day."

The man was holding out something to him, a piece of letter

paper, folded, sealed. He reached and took it. "Thank you." And unprompted, without the conscious effort of these last days, "Sir."

"No thanks needed. It gave me an excuse to grab a breath of fresh air." The man nodded at him and was gone and Jared Heath, warmed by a brief, unblemished contact with his kind, stepped to the brighter light of the doorway holding the letter and turned it over and in the instant of turning knew the hand that had written. With a feeling of inevitability, of relentless, onward movement, he broke the seal and unfolded the paper. There was no salutation, only the lines in his father's small, shaken, yet unshakable script.

I regard it as a blessing that your grandfather did not live to see this day—It is my duty to inform you that your cowardly desertion is common knowledge in the town. The shock has confined your mother to her bed and the doctors hold out no hope for her. Your brother is shunned by his former playmates. As for myself, if I were younger, I would instantly enlist to do all possible to wipe away some of the disgrace you have brought upon the family— upon the name you bear. I would take that name from you if I could. I can only state that this is the last you will ever hear from any of us

He leaned against the sagging doorjamb and stared down at the paper in his hands, a man in the dusty, stiff, ill-fitting uniform of a private leaning against the rotted doorjamb of a rickety shed behind an old barn in the backwash of a forgotten battle in northern Virginia, and there was no outward alteration in him and yet he altered, imperceptibly, facing inward away from the past and all that it had meant and might mean. Slowly he refolded the paper and ran his fingers along the creases to tighten them. Slowly he took a small, leather-laced account book from the pocket of his jacket and opened it and placed the folded paper between its pages and closed it and put it again in the pocket. Slowly, steadily, he moved out from the shed doorway and along the rear of the barn and in through the open, wide doorway there and pulled down hay from the low loft and gathered a big bundle in his arms and returned outside with this and dropped it in front of the tired mules. Slowly, steadily, he took a pair of old, heavy brushes that hung fastened together with a piece of cord looped over a nail on a post of the picket line and with regular strokes, a brush in each hand, began to rub down the first of the mules. In all outward appearance there had been no break, only a slight interruption, in his patient, plodding endurance of the routine of present duty, and yet there had been a break, complete, distinct, in the man himself, as inevitable perhaps and as relentless as the pressures that had been beating upon him. He knew without any knowing that could be translated into words, that needed any translation into exact thought, that he had come to the end of one road and had faced along another that had no direction as yet and no destination, only a purpose whose ultimate grasping alone could give significance to continued existence.

It was with no sensation of surprise that he looked up from his work and saw the figure standing a few feet away, watching him, slim and slight, eyes tired and yet somehow alert and eager above the still incredibly neat, untainted uniform of an army major.

"Heath," said Major Foster. "Jared Heath. I have been looking for you. You can forget those mules. You are my responsibility now."

He remains a strange figure, not too clearly seen, this Matthew Foster, a representative in the field of the judge advocate general's office created earlier in the war by special act of Congress. To use his own words reversed upon him, it would be interesting to know more of his background. But that would be to go astray on a side trail. No man's actions, what he is and what he does, are determined solely by himself alone; they are shaped and slanted by the endless countless impacts of circumstances and the acts and beings of others about him, touching him, impinging upon him. An attempt to understand Matthew Foster in satisfactory completeness would lead on, as the story of Jared Heath has led to him, to the necessity of trying to understand others and other circumstances that helped make and motivate him. It is enough, it has to be enough, to know that he was essentially a civilian, an intelligent, firm-principled lawyer out of New York, a man who did not abdicate independent individuality when he donned a uniform, who could comprehend and faithfully do his duty under wartime military procedure without fully approving that procedure. It is possible to speculate, even to be reasonably certain, that he was prompted, in the actions that impinged upon Jared Heath, by some instinctive sense of his own of expiation for his own role in the relentless, perhaps not remorseless yet still relentless, waste of warfare.

It is even possible to speculate that perhaps, had there been no Matthew Foster, Jared Heath might still somehow, somewhere, sometime have found the way, a way, for himself. Or through the impinging upon him of some other man or men or combination of circumstances. But the fact stands that it was this Matthew Foster, whatever his precise personal motives, who interfered, respectful of regulations and careful to obtain proper authority, though no official records seem to have been kept or at least preserved of the interference, with the ordained routine of military justice and pointed him, Jared Heath, along a new path that would lead at last to another bloody hillside fifteen hundred miles away in the rugged, arid reaches of the Texas Panhandle.

He sat on an empty, upturned nailkeg in the inner room of a small two-room shanty on the edge of the crossroads settlement that had been taken over as corps headquarters. A canvas cot with a neatly folded blanket, a chair, a table with a few books and many papers: this was Major Foster's field office. In the outer room, visible through the open doorway between, two uniformed clerks monotonously copied records for the evening dispatches northeastward to Washington. He sat on the upturned keg and waited, quiet in the patience that was not a patience, doing what he had been told to do, which was to wait here.

Footsteps from outside sounded coming through the front room. He raised his head and saw Major Foster in the inner doorway, entering, closing the door, and he rose from the keg, stiffening to attention.

"Sit down, Heath, sit down." Major Foster crossed to the table and swung around to lean back against the edge. The bare trace of a tired, quizzical smile flickered on the lean, clean-shaven face. "As I remember saying to you once before, we can dispense with the formalities."

The tone, the trace of a smile caught, seized with an eagerness that startled him, cut into the shell of endurance he held about him, and deliberately he rebuilt against a break and waited.

"I imagine you have been wondering what this is all about."

"No." It was a simple statement of fact.

"No? What kind of a man are you?"

An answer was expected, required. Again it was a simple statement of fact. "I'm a man who has been convicted of cowardice."

Major Foster slapped his hands on the table edge and rocked back and then forward, bent forward, earnest, intent. "Still wrapped in yourself, aren't you, Heath. Listen to me. See if you can get this into that hard, Yankee head of yours. To me, right now, you are not a coward. You are not a brave man either. I don't know what you are. But you are another human being. And you worry me . . . Not you. Not the thick-skulled hulk of meat and bone that is you squatted there behind some kind of a wall you have erected for yourself. No! But what you represent . . . Do you think you are the only one? Day after day, every day, the same thing happens all through the corps. Men, maybe good men, crushed, ruined, by some sudden set of circumstances, some pressure that is too much for them. So they are tried, convicted, junked. I grant that it may be necessary. But it is also damnably wasteful. Does a single cowardly act make a man a coward? Yes. For that moment. But how about the brave acts that may be in his record? Do they not make him a hero? Yes. For those moments. On which should his life stand? And the whole damned, dirty, wasteful business has to pass through my hands . . ."

Major Foster looked down at his trim, dusty boots, studying them, and Jared Heath watched him, still remote, still safe behind his wall, yet aware that a part of himself was raw, quivering with the ache of something almost forgotten, of being confronted by a man who spoke to him, mind to mind, out of all reason and rank, and abruptly Major Foster looked up again. "I'm a fool, Heath. But I would think less of myself if I were not . . . Would you like a chance to redeem yourself?"

Honesty, stripped honesty only, with this slim slight man who had closed a door shutting out the army, the war, the whole rest of the world, shutting the two of them in, and was driving him to grapple in words with what for himself needed no words.

"No." And after a moment, "That means nothing to me now."

"And what does?"

"To know," said Jared Heath. And again, breaking through, rushing, intense: "To know! Just that! For myself! Really know!"

There it was, there it is, the one approach the man ever made, or at least can be gleaned from his own detached impersonal accounts and the scant material available about him, to putting into words the solitary purpose he had wrung out of all that had happened to him. To know. Just that. He had been pushed past all possible leaning on the opinion, the judgment, even the sympathy or the understanding, of others or another, on to the final bulwark of individual being, to sole, single reliance upon his own judgment of himself. And he did not know.

And if he did not know, how could Matthew Foster know? A strange figure he remains, this Matthew Foster, because he did know, or thought he knew, pushed in his turn by the driving necessity of a knowing to buttress, to support, to make possible and to excuse the decision already made, the course of action already outlined, in his own mind.

There was a silence in that shut-off inner room of that small shanty where two men stared unseeing at the same essential problem from the opposite poles of their pasts and what these had made them and where these had placed them, one low on an empty, upturned keg, head dropped now between slumped shoulders, the other upright, leaning against the edge of a dusty, littered table.

"Heath," said Major Foster, quietly, gently. "I think that at bottom we are both talking about the same thing . . ." He put his hands on the table edge and hitched himself up to sitting upon it and placed his hands on his knees and leaned forward, watching the slumped figure down and across from him, and spoke again, impersonal now, speaking perhaps in the manner that had been and would be again so effective in his civilian legal career, precise, ironical, with an irony that could give no offense because it somehow included himself in its cool comprehension of the folly inherent in human existence.

"I have requested and obtained authority to select from my files a small number of men like yourself, line officers who have been reduced to the ranks. Busted, I believe, is the usual term. They will comprise a very mixed group because this is, quite frankly, an experiment. The purpose is to give them a chance to—I will change the word—to prove themselves again in battle. They are to be organized into a separate unit, hardly more than a squad, I should say, since the number is limited to eight, though some wag in Washington has already officially designated it as Company Q. That letter, I take from his sarcastic comments, stands for queer, quixotic. I might add that the whole notion has also been labeled, among other things, as Foster's Foolishness. I accept the implication. Until the unit is organized and I find a place for it in some active regiment, I am personally responsible for it . . . Perhaps the company designation is, after all, technically correct, because it is to remain a unit, however small, under its own officer. As its temporary commander, I will give what help I can, which will be very little because of the pressure of my regular duties and because I am lamentably ignorant of regular army routine. I suspect that the best I can do for this still nonexistent orphan outfit is to try to give it the right man. I am convinced he should be one of them himself. Obviously no commission can be involved, so he must be a sergeant. I am offering you that doubtful and perhaps unenviable distinction."

Slowly Jared Heath stiffened, had been stiffening, his head rising, and for the first time in long days he looked straight through the shell of endurance about him into the eyes of another man. A forlorn anger and a kind of anguish trembled along the frayed fringe of his voice. "You say I am not the only one. Why do you choose me?"

"Because you are unique, Heath. In my experience at least. You had no defense and true enough, in all recognizable fact, you had none and you said so and you made no effort to scratch up excuses. For some reason I do not quite understand yet that means something to me."

There was a silence again in that shut-off room and from beyond the closed door came the sound of stools scraping on the floor and from outside by the roadway the tread of tramping feet and the rumble of heavy wagons and these were removed, shut out, meaningless to the silence in that room, and abruptly Major Foster pushed out from the table edge. "Well, Heath, do you accept my offer?"

Slowly he rose upright from the squat, low keg, shoulders instinctively squaring, a soldier in the ill-fitting, stiff, blue uniform of a private struggling against the inescapable fact, beyond reason, beyond logic, that he could accept nothing, not even from this man, and an unwilled appeal ran now with the anger and the anguish along the faltering fringe of his voice. "I would prefer, sir, that it be an order."

Slim, slight, unforgettable in this only the second and yet the last but for one brief, inconclusive, later time Jared Heath would ever see the man, ever have contact with him except through a few written notes and his own reports during the next few days, Major Foster stared at him, studying him, and there flickered in the man's eyes a flash of understanding, again beyond reason, beyond logic, perhaps of pride in some obscure, grasped but unidentifiable, justification of judgment.

"Very well, Heath. I will make it an order."

Three

That too was a beginning. Not of a battle, not of anything that would echo later in history. Simply the beginning, insignificant against the swirling panorama of the war, almost unnoticed except by the few directly involved, of a queer, quixotic experiment with a small orphan outfit. And here, in northern Virginia, in the backwash of the fighting around Spotsylvania Court House, it never became more than a beginning, was thwarted, tossed aside, soon all but forgotten and eventually erased from whatever records there might have been.

A man named Matthew Foster summoned that beginning into being. That can be known, is known. What it cost him in persistence, in argument, in persuasion, perhaps in maneuvering of political pressure, cannot be known. Nor what too it may have meant to him when a limitation he had to accept in order to make that beginning canceled it later for him, not out of existence, but insofar as he could foresee for the purpose he had in mind. All that is lost with the notes which, if he ever made them on this experiment, he must have destroyed. There remain in tangible evidence only two sheets of plain paper with lines in his neat, precise script preserved beside a carefully creased letter in an old leather-laced account book.

It is not even possible to be certain whether Matthew Foster ever learned what became of his beginning months and many miles away in the Texas Panhandle. There is a chance, perhaps even a probability, that he did. Certainly he should have because he was the one man who knew Jared Heath along the far way who might have fully understood it.

The war had become almost one long, sustained battle now, every day, every night marked by fighting somewhere along the front. The Union forces, unable to break through around Spotsylvania, not even in a powerful, day-long massed assault at the Bloody Angle, were beginning the shifting, sidling movement southeastward that would underline other names indelibly into history: the North Anna River, Cold Harbor, Petersburg. And behind the lines, behind the little crossroads settlement that was temporary corps headquarters, surrounded by the vast endless activity of replacement troops and supplies moving up to the front, yet isolated from it, in a cleared corner of a small woodlot too small for any other use, screened by fencerow brambles, a man named Jared Heath established his camp.

He had nothing, only the ill-fitting uniform of a private he wore. Only that and a requisition form that would enable him to draw daily rations as needed for eight men and an envelope handed him, sealed, by one of the clerks at the door of Major Foster's office in the early hours of the morning. He sat now cross-legged on the ground, where he had spent the night, in this spot he had picked, beside his small morning fire. He broke the seal and opened the envelope.

Obstacles already, Heath. I find that until you are attached to some regiment you can be issued no equipment. Meanwhile you

will have to make out as best you can. Your men should be report-
ing to you today. The enclosed listing is simply for your informa-
tion. You are to use your own judgment in handling these men.
You have a job to do and you are to do it. That is an order. I might
add it is the only order I feel competent to give you.

MATTHEW FOSTER

It occurs to me, in regard to equipment, that your temporary com-
mander is much too busy a man to ask any questions concerning
any items you happen to acquire.

He read this once, twice. He stared down at it, no longer seeing it,
for a long time. He stirred and opened the envelope again and
took out the other paper. He sat quiet, studying this. Carefully he
folded the two papers over to size and took from his jacket pocket
a small, leather-laced account book and opened it and placed the
two papers between its pages and closed it and returned it to the
pocket. He rose and went over along the near fence line and
hunted among the brambles until he found a piece of old, weath-
ered board and returned and sat again by the fading fire. He
pulled a small stick from the embers and with the blackened,
charred end began to trace letters on the board: COMPANY Q.

Merriam, Alfred: Formerly lieutenant, an Ohio regiment—
enlisted at seventeen—lied about age—three years' service—
breveted at Antietam—dropped out of first day's fighting present
campaign, minor wound in foot—convicted on doctor's testimony
it must have been self-inflicted—own account highly improba-
ble—inconsistent in cross-examination.

He stood by the sagging, broken, old rail fence that separated the
woodlot from the unused lane running past it. He was fastening

his board to the top rail with a length of rusty wire when he saw the man approaching, limping, favoring the left foot, stocky farm-bred body bulging the too small, insignia-stripped, seam-split uniform of an infantry private. He watched the man, the boy, young, unbelievably young and beaten behind the hardened exterior of a rushed, telescoped maturity, stop and stare at the lettered board and then at him.

"I'm alookin' for Sergeant Heath."

"You've found him."

He saw the dark flush climbing up the other's face, heard the sullen defiance creeping into the voice. "Now lookahere, mister. I've took about all I'm agoin' to take these last days. Where's he at?"

He was aware of his own raw rankless jacket and of his position, remote, ridiculous, in the midst of an army at war, holding a partially-fastened, old board in place along a sagging rail, aware too of the final deliberate commitment in the words, and his voice was quiet, steady. "I am Sergeant Heath."

The other stared at him, stiffening. "I'm Merriam."

"I figured you were." He leaned down and finished fastening the board and straightened again. The other was still staring at him.

"Major Foster says I'm to take orders from you. Well, you got any?"

"Yes . . . How's the foot?"

He saw the flush leaping now up the other's face and he spoke again. "I mean, are you able to get around on it all right?"

"I got here."

"Good. You head a couple hundred yards east of here, across the next field, and you hit a road. Troops were moving there last night. Green troops. A long way and they were mighty tired.

They'll have been shedding stuff. The quartermaster crews can't have found it all yet. You backtrack along there and find me a knapsack."

"Knapsack?"

"Look, Merriam. We haven't a damn thing. Nobody will be giving us a thing. The first we need is a knapsack. You go get it."

"Supposin' I don't come back?"

"You'll be back. With a knapsack."

He saw the eyes wavering, steadying, the sullen lines of the mouth firming. He watched the stocky figure, young, pathetically young, beaten, step over the lone, low rail of a break in the fence and start across the woodlot toward the field beyond, hesitant, irresolute, and stop and turn back. And suddenly, even before he heard the voice, hoarse, hurried, breaking into this with a rush, he knew that here it was, dragged into the open at the start by the first of them, what would scatter and damn them all or would hold them together for whatever was to come.

"I got to tell someone! I'm no good anywhere anymore! They were right! I did it! I picked up a gun and shot myself!"

He heard his own voice, quiet, steady, stating a fact. "So did I, Merriam. The only difference is I didn't use a gun." And after a moment, another fact. "And now we need a knapsack."

He watched the stocky, young figure move off, limping, favoring the left foot, moving straight toward the distant road, and he felt a flicker of wry, ironic interest in himself, that he should be standing by a sagging, old rail fence holding to a few words, meaningless to the hard base of his being now, yet held as if worth the holding. "Thank you, sir."

Selous, Owen: Formerly captain New Jersey regiment—state militia taken into army—good record precious campaigns—left his command somewhere in woods, found later wandering behind lines—claimed he lost contact in the confusion—cracked under questioning and admitted panic—"went to pieces" his exact phrase.

Geary, Silas: Was a lieutenant Connecticut regiment—second year of service—in advance bivouac three nights ago—hit by sudden raid, enemy probably after prisoners for questioning—apparently thought it real attack and ran for rear—claimed he was sure camp was taken and he one of last left—evidence indicates he was one of the first awakened—raid quickly repelled by others remaining.

He sat again on the ground, cross-legged, by the now dead fire. Across his thighs lay a knapsack. Another and a haversack and two canteens lay on the ground beside him. A few yards away Private Merriam sat on a small log, left shoe off, examining the adhesive bandage around the foot.

"Damn good thing," said Private Merriam, "these shoes a couple sizes too big."

He looked up and over. "If you slit the shoe down the toe it might feel easier."

"Yep," said Private Merriam. "If I had somethin' to slit with."

He unfastened the knapsack across his thighs and fumbled inside and found it, a straight-edge razor, blade folded into the handle. He tossed this to Private Merriam. He reached inside again and took out a piece of cloth rolled into a somewhat flattened, cylindrical bundle, the standard kit known as the army man's housewife. He unrolled this, exposing the articles within, each tucked into its own little pocket: a pair of scissors, a sponge, a comb, a small flat brush. He shook his head slightly and rolled up the cloth and tucked it into the knapsack and set this aside and took the other. Again he held a housewife in his hands and unrolled the cloth and as it unrolled a small object fell out, a spool of dark thread with a needle stuck through it, and he retrieved this and laid it carefully aside and took the scissors out of their little pocket and set the housewife and knapsack on the ground beside him. Leaning forward, he cut a thin strip from around the bottom of each leg of his light blue pants. He held these up, two thin circlets of light blue cloth, and cut each into three parts, six short strips in all. He set these and the scissors on the ground and unbuttoned his jacket and pulled it off and laid it across his lap with the left sleeve up and reached for the spool of thread.

He was sewing the third strip, the last chevron on the left sleeve, above the elbow, points down, when Private Merriam spoke. "Sorry to bother you, Sergeant, but more's arrivin'."

He looked up and around and saw the two men stepping over the lone rail of the break in the fence and approaching, together and yet not exactly together, a restraint, a separateness, apparent between them as if they had already measured each other and moved apart, not in distance but in mutual, inner withdrawal, the one late-middle-aged, thickening at the waist, beginning to sag at the shoulders, eyes tired and deep-sunk over prominent nose and short, square-cut beard, the other younger, much younger, slender, erect, and easy in movement, a suggestion of defiance in the swing of shoulders and set expression of lean, fine-featured face. They stopped and looked down at him and the jacket across his lap. It was the older man who spoke, hearty, too hearty, the forced quality slipping past control.

"You must be Heath. Sergeant Heath."

"Yes.

"I'm Selous. Owen Selous. A peculiar name but mine own.

Private Owen Selous, I should say. Reporting for duty as per instructions from our mutual friend Foster. Major Foster. This gentleman with me—"

"Hold it." He stuck the needle into the cloth and put his arms back, hands flat on the ground, looking up. "Here each man speaks for himself."

The younger man stared down at him, deliberately waiting, not long, just long enough to establish an interval, an independence. He spoke, short, precise, clipping the words. "Geary. Silas Geary." A pause. "Private Silas Geary."

"Well, now, what do you think." The older man was talking again, hearty again, too hearty, pushed by some need to make himself, his presence, known and apparent. "Neither one of us thought to say 'sir.' Habit, I suppose. Former rank, you know. I'm wondering, Sergeant, are you going to be a stickler on such things?"

He heard himself speaking, quiet, steady, a trace of remembered irony in his tone. "I think we can dispense with the formalities."

"Good. Very good. Not that I object but I seem to be forgetful these days. Can't seem to—"

He broke in. "Except, perhaps, when we are engaged in company activities. Roll call, drilling—"

It was the younger man who started a bit, surprised, perhaps indignant. "Drilling?"

"Certainly. We are still in the army. No active field duty at the moment. None even in sight yet. I believe Major Foster would say we are in training."

"Of course." The older man was pushing in again. "We need it. All of us no doubt rusty at things like that. And there's something I want to have straight. Right now, at the start. Don't expect too much of me. No illusions about myself anymore. I'm a cracked crock. Wouldn't have thought it a week ago. But things got hot and mixed up and went on so long I cracked. Went to pieces. No other way to put it. just went to pieces. Only practical thing to do in a case like that is face it. Accept it. I'm a man who goes to pieces. Then that major sends for me and says maybe, since I know that now, I can find a way to stick the pieces together a bit tighter. I don't think so. A man is what he is. But I figured I might as well give it a whirl. Better anyway than what I was doing, unloading supply wagons all day."

He leaned back, looking up, aware of the hurt-scarred bewilderment far back in the tired eyes belying the bluff, forced heartiness of manner, and the thought pressed that now, at this moment, he should say something and there was nothing in him to say, and the man pushed on. "Now Geary here is different. He's still mad. Still thinks they pegged him wrong. Can't admit that maybe he funked it too. Can't see the practical thing is—"

"Quit that!"

He watched the younger man swing back from the other to him, concentrating on him. "I put it to you, sir! The first real sleep I had in days! I come awake all at once hearing shots all around! I scramble out of the damned, little dog tent thing I had! It's almighty dark and all I can see is one of our men running like hell away and another just going down! How'd I know it was only a couple of our pickets pushed back? Not another of our men in sight anywhere! Not a single one I tell you! How'd I know how long it'd been going on? And a whole bunch of those goddamned, gray-coat rebs coming in, overrunning the place! Anybody'd think the rest of the outfit had pulled back somewhere to make a stand! So I went looking for them! I wasn't running away! I was looking for them! Can you understand that?"

"I don't know. I'll be honest with you, Geary. I don't care. I don't care what you thought. What you did. All I care about, and that not much, is what you do here."

He still leaned back and looked up at the two of them studying him, assessing what he had said, and this too was ridiculous—he low leaning back against the ground looking up, bare-armed with a stiff, wrinkled jacket across his lap, and he should be erect, on his feet, taking charge, some dignity in the situation, and that was unnecessary because he was not leaning back against the firmness of the earth alone but against the hard rock of resolution within himself. He heard his own voice, quiet, steady. "We're here now. No equipment will be issued for a while. What we get we must get ourselves. Merriam here has made a start. What you see. We'll be needing tents. This dry weather can't hold forever and we don't know how long we'll be here. Tents. Does either of you have an idea on that?"

He waited. It was the younger man who spoke at last, unwilling, distant, but speaking. "An outfit near ours got pretty well scrambled a few days back. In camp. Some reb artillery got in close and had the range. Chances are it's not cleaned up yet. What's left is probably all ripped apart but you might do something with it."

"You mean 'we' might, don't you, Geary?"

He sensed, could almost feel, the man swinging without moving to confront the fact before him, and he heard the soft sigh of breath drawing in, held, being released, and the low words. "Yes. I suppose I do."

"That's it then. You two go see what you can find."

It was the older man who hesitated, starting away with the other and turning back. "I like to have things straight and tidy, Sergeant. Who is in command of this little expedition?"

"Geary."

He saw the slight tremor of shock, of disappointment, in the man's face, the awareness of a subtle affront to former rank, to age, to seniority, and he spoke again. "It was his suggestion." And again he sensed, faint, yet unmistakably there, the movement within to confront a fact that was more than a fact.

"Yes," said Private Owen Selous. "I see what you mean. It was his."

He turned his head to watch the two men moving off, stepping over the lone rail of the break in the fence to the lane, not together, apart in mutual withdrawal, and yet together, side by side, and he turned back at the sound of footsteps a few yards away.

"Yep," said Private Merriam. "This shoe feels better. We'll be needin' more of this stuff I brought. If you don't mind, sir, I'll take me another little trip."

Webb, Joseph: Formerly captain a New York regiment—three years' service, none previous in field—garrison duty somewhere—assigned to regiment when organized early this year— men broke under first heavy fire and he broke with them—suggestion he set example—claimed he thought he saw the major waving them back in retreat—a remarkably frantic retreat by most accounts—and fact was established the major had been killed shortly before.

Fulton, James: Subaltern same regiment as above—drafted from good civilian job—no attempt to dodge or buy off—earned his post in training—but didn't even come under fire—dropped out in the advance—said he had a sudden call of nature—but two impartial witnesses saw him well back, in hiding, breaking open cartridges and smearing powder on his face.

He had finished the right sleeve too and was up, jacket on, pacing slowly, checking the ground slope and drainage of the woodlot corner, when he saw the two men coming toward him. He stopped and waited for them to approach, the one in the lead stout, thickset, erect in bearing, head high, a faint disdainful expression on wide-mustached face, the other lagging behind, following, younger in outline but with little trace of youth left in slouching sag of tired muscles and perhaps of even more tired spirit, simply the outward semblance of a man with all that might be individual drawn inward, hidden, unreadable behind fixed mask of it face.

They halted, holding their relative positions, and the one in the lead looked him over, gaze lingering on the improvised stripes on his sleeves, lips curling slightly under the wide mustache.

"You Heath?"

"Yes."

"I'm Joseph Webb. I'll speak my piece and shut up. I don't like this, any of it. I don't belong here. Not me. A raw miscarriage of justice. They give me poor men. A bunch of bounty bastards and the scrapings of prisons. No officer could lick them into shape. First time they hear bullets flying they cut and run. What's a man to do when his outfit's collapsed? Stand out there alone and be shot? Then a bunch of staff men who don't know what it is out on the line sit in judgment. Give me some good men and I'd show them. I don't like this. But an order's an order and I don't see any other way to get a chance to prove my point. I'll do what I'm told but I don't have to like it. Do you follow me?"

"Yes." He shifted a bit toward the other man. "And you?"

Even the voice was blank, conveying nothing but the bare information. "James Fulton." He waited. There was nothing more.

He was aware of movement off to one side. Private Merriam

was approaching, empty-handed, disheveled, limp very noticeable. The young face was flushed, sullen.

"I had more stuff, sir. But bumped into a quartermaster crew and the sonsabitches took it."

"Did they try to arrest you?"

The head rose higher and he caught the brief glint in the eyes. "Yep. But they wasn't much good in the brush."

"The fortunes of war, Merriam. Forget it now." He was conscious of the other two watching, hearing, the one interested, intent, lips curling again under the wide mustache, the other blank, hidden, unknowable, and he ignored them, concentrating on Merriam. "See that level stretch along the fence? We'll put the tents there. You can get started clearing away those briers."

The glint was there again, brief but caught. "You really expect them back, sir? With anything?"

"They'll be back. With something. Even if Selous has to rip some canvas from right over some general's head." And suddenly it was there, in him, not meaning much to the essential hardness of self, but there, a hope that what he had said was true, that what he had said simply because it was the thing to say, because he had an order to obey and he was obeying it, would be true.

Private Merriam moved away and he turned to the other two men. "We'll be needing a sink. In that lower corner behind those bushes is a likely spot. I don't know how long we'll be here so I want it plenty deep. Smoothed around with a pile of loose dirt at one end for daily covering. You two can tackle that."

They stood motionless, staring at him, and the stout man's lips, not curling now, tightened into a straight taut line. He spoke slowly. "I'll do it, Heath. But I insist upon knowing something. Is there anything personal in giving us the dirty job?"

"No job is dirty here, Webb. Unless they all are. But at least

73

they are all the same. We'll have rations. Other men are out after shelter. Sanitary provisions come next."

Slowly the stout man nodded. "I follow you on that." The head stopped moving, erect, the chin thrust forward. "Shovels. We can't dig without shovels."

"The army has shovels, Webb. Plenty of them. All around. Burial crews, earthworks, road repairs. I don't give a damn how or where you get them . . . We can use an ax too."

Abruptly the stout man turned away and started toward the lane and the other, silent, mechanical, turned to follow, and something in the pattern there nudged his mind. "Fulton!"

Both men stopped, the stout man in the lead with head half turned, the other shifting slowly around.

"You've tagged long enough. Go on down to that corner and start laying it out. Webb can get the tools."

The man's eyes met his for an instant, direct, straight on, and flicked aside, and the slouching figure moved around and past him toward the lower corner of the woodlot.

The stout man was full turned now, facing him, all trace of disdain gone from the wide-mustached face. "You want me to do this alone, don't you, Heath?"

"That's right."

"You're a shrewd man, Heath . . . But you're wrong." And abruptly again the stout figure, erect, head high, was striding toward the lane.

Kinsey, Stewart: Formerly lieutenant Pennsylvania regiment— Philadelphia to be exact—commission in State militia, taken into army—probably political appointment at start—nondescript record—let himself be captured two days ago—"recaptured" when enemy position taken before he was sent to rear—according to

enemy prisoners he voluntarily surrendered, came in and gave
himself up—probably had exchange parole in mind—just
unlucky in a way—suspect others have got away with that partic-
ular trick.

There was activity now in the small, isolated woodlot. At one end
of the level stretch along the fence Privates Selous and Geary were
pegging down the first low tent, made of ragged strips of canvas
pieced together. Nearby Private Merriam sat on the ground, left
shoe off patiently pulling threads from the frayed edge of another
strip of canvas to be used in stitching still others together. A battered coffeepot hung on a tripod of three short poles over a fire
rebuilt on the remains of the previous one. From the lower corner
of the lot behind the bushes came the sound of shovels striking
into dirt.

He was resting briefly, leaning on an ax, a pile of trimmed saplings for tent poles by his feet, when he saw the man sitting on the
top rail of the old fence by the entrance break. Seen now, aware of
being seen, the man pushed out and landed lightly on booted feet
and came forward, slim, tall, well-proportioned, still in the dark
blue pants and longish coat of an officer from which all identifying
insignia had been removed. There was a slight, twisted smile on
the handsome face, self-sufficient, self-contained, a suggestion of
insolence, perhaps not so much insolence as indifference to anyone
and anything, in the bearing.

"Sergeant Heath, I suppose."

"Yes."

"Stewart Kinsey, late of the 106th Pennsylvania, at your service."
The handsome head cocked at a slight angle and a kind of sardonic
humor showed in the eyes. "A hell of an outfit you have here, Sergeant. What I can see. And it's a hell of a war too. Started out fair

enough, to preserve the Union. Then Lincoln got too big for his backwoods britches and issued that silly proclamation. Free the niggers. Nonsense. Who in his senses'll fight to do that? And it develops into a slugging match that likely won't accomplish anything but ruin the whole country anyway. So I tried to step out of it. Got nipped back. You might say I had an easy break being slapped with cowardice instead of desertion but I had that angle figured which was why I did it my way. So I come wandering over here."

"Why here?"

"Well, it seems I had a choice, Sergeant. Put to me very neatly. Sweat for the quartermaster or try this. Choice of evils, you might say. You ought to be complimented I picked you. And the first thing I see here is men working. Apparently I just can't avoid it. I suppose you expect to be putting me to work?"

"That's right."

"Ah, well . . . What kind of work, Sergeant?"

He studied the tall, neat figure a moment, conscious of Merriam a dozen feet away on the ground, listening, of Selous and Geary evidently busy with their pegs, but listening too. "Blankets, Kinsey. We need blankets. Everything we get we have to find for ourselves. About a third to a half-mile west of here there's an ambulance depot. Farmhouse. Barn. Behind that barn there's a pile of blankets thrown out as too messed and filthy for further use. Probably not burned yet. Soak them enough and scrub them enough and some of them might be serviceable."

The slight smile was still on the man's face, deepened now, humorless. "Hospital blankets, eh? You're smart, Sergeant. Didn't take you long to think up that one. Just for me."

"Not just for you. It happens to be next on my list." He felt a flash of sardonic amusement of his own. "But I'm not sorry that it happens to be next."

"Ah, yes. I sometimes affect people that way . . . And suppose I refuse?"

"I'll chuck you right back to the quartermaster." The words were spoken and in the instant of speaking he knew they were wrong.

The smile was still there on the handsome face, definitely mocking now. "And count it good riddance, eh, Sergeant? But that would upset the good, little major's nice, little applecart. I don't think you'd quite do that."

He waited, aware that he had let control of the situation slip away, that nothing he might say could change it. And far back in the other's eyes he saw a glint, a gleam, unfathomable, and he heard the other's voice, still gently mocking. "Ah, well, Sergeant, perhaps you underestimate me . . . West did you say? About a half-mile?"

Zattig, Hugo: I break my rule on this man—he held no commission—was a sergeant in Indiana regiment—stretch in the army before the war—signed again the first week—has been busted several times before, drunkenness, insubordination—was in that peculiar demonstration second day's fighting current campaign when whole brigade simply quit and started back—not exactly a retreat, just walking out of it—rest were stopped and rallied but he went right on—understand it took a scuffle to stop him and get him under control—I send him to you, Heath, because I think you and Company Q need a little luck.

Late afternoon sun slanted through the trees along the far side of the lane across the level space along the rail fence where Privates Selous and Geary worked on the fourth tent. Close by the fire Private Merriam unpacked rations from a burlap bag. A few yards away Privates Webb and Fulton, weary, dirt-smudged, lay stretched on the ground staring up at the sky, shovels beside them. Beyond, at the edge of the small clearing, Private Kinsey, coat off, naked to the waist, was hanging wet blankets on a rope strung between two trees.

He leaned against the fence by the entrance break, looking along the lane. There was no one in sight. From the distance, remote, from another world, came the low, reverberating rumble of artillery batteries in action. He let his head drop, staring down unseeing at the ground just beyond the fence.

He raised his head. The man had approached quite near, surprisingly quiet for all the seeming huge bulk silhouetted against the sunlight shafts through the laneside trees. He raised his head higher, the visor of his forage cap shading his eyes, and watched the approaching figure, seen closer now large but no longer huge, tall, wide-sloping-shouldered, thick-chested, flat-bellied, flat-shanked, long arms dangling low, long legs moving in easy, loose-jointed stride. It swung angling toward him and he could make out the face, broad and flat, stubble-bearded, hard, stubborn, not flesh but chipped stone.

"Heath?"

"Yes.

"Zattig." The man faced him across the fence, feet a bit apart, solid on them. An impression of simple strength and individual immovability came to him, known before in another man, grasped now, unmistakable. The voice was slightly nasal, slightly drawling. "I been thinkin', sir. Made up me mind. To tell ye about meself. Back there some in the brush I had me enough of this fool war. No point chewin' reasons. It's been run fool-like from the start. Made up me mind. That's me way. That's why they busted me this time."

"Then why are you here?"

The big head nodded, slow, taking the question. "I was comin' to that. Made up me mind again. To see it through. The hitch I signed for. That major says somethin'. Says maybe it is a fool war but I didn't run out on it, I run out on meself. I been thinkin'. Made up me mind he's right."

He studied the man, wary now after the thin, scraping, past disaster with Kinsey, wondering how to take hold of this, and there was no need to wonder, because the man himself, without moving, simply by speaking again, was reaching out to him. "The major says to watch out for ye, Sarge. A hard man, he says. Rub ye the wrong way, he says, and ye'll have me hide. That so?"

He heard his own voice, unprompted, in the tone almost forgotten, the manner thought never to be regained, crisp, incisive, stating a suddenly established fact. "You're goddamned eternally right I will."

He saw the slow smile spreading across the broad face, the slow nod, the acceptance reaching beyond rank, beyond authority, and then the man was looking past him at the cleared corner of the woodlot and the other men scattered there. "The major says we can't draw stuff for a while. Seems like I'm late. Seems like them others been earnin' rations. Reckon I better earn me own. Ye figure on makin' it a fightin' unit?"

"That's what the major has in mind."

"I reckoned so. Guns now. We be needin' them. Supposin' I crawl off an' snaffle a few. That rub ye wrong?"

"Only if you fail to get them."

Again he saw the slow smile, a warmth stirring on the hard, chipped flatness of the face, and the man turned, awkward yet not awkward, slack power sliding in the loose-jointed frame, and started away along the lane.

"Zattig!"

The man stopped, shifting a little to swing his head and look back.

"Don't get caught getting them."

The man's eyes met his and an ache, sudden and sharp, beat down through him at the words. "Don't ye go frettin' any, Sarge. I take a lot a catchin'. I been in an' out a this fool army so much I know me way around."

Four

Eight men in a small, isolated woodlot. Seven other men and Jared Heath, in the midst of a war yet out of it, their only tie to it now a slender, neat man in a major's uniform somehow finding time in his busy, endless movement throughout the corps to ask colonel after colonel the question that could determine their destiny.

Three days in that woodlot, three days with the war beginning to draw off into the distance in the shifting, sidling movement southeastward, three eternities perhaps to those eight men themselves with the long moments dragging despite the innumerable, petty activities of shaking themselves and improvised pieced-out equipment into possible serviceable shape. It would be interesting, it would add to understanding of what happened later, if those moments could be filled in fully, more known of the frictions and inevitable flarings-up and the gropings toward fellowship of those eight men thrown together out of all normal reason and ordinary circumstance, each crippled in his own way, each carrying his own individual convicted past and his own reaction to it into a temporarily shared and unforeseeable future. Available now are only the scant, impersonalized memories of one of them, of Jared Heath, told in the long, late years when the garrulousness of age was on him, the memories of an old man looking far, far back into what was virtually another existence, few and brief, yet somehow adding up to something that prompted him, in the evening of the third day, to make the decision that did determine their destiny . . .

Seven men at the moment, in the early evening of the first day. Six other men and Jared Heath. One of them was still out somewhere in the dusk, moving silently in long, loose-jointed stride despite seeming huge bulk.

He stood off to the side watching them by the fire, Merriam upright, stirring the contents of an old bucket that hung by the battered coffeepot over the fire, the others down, sitting or stretched on the ground, waiting. They were quiet, too quiet. The silence, the absence of sound, was a pressure over them.

Faintly, from down the lane, he heard a jingle, a soft tapping of metal on metal. He moved over to the rail fence, by the entrance break, and saw the figure approaching, strange in the dimming half-light, bulky, misshapen. It came closer and he made out Private Zattig, a bundle of rifles under each arm, a string of cartridge boxes on a rope around his neck and down over each shoulder.

"Got 'em, Sarge," said Private Zattig, low-toned, matter of fact. "Ten rounds apiece too."

"Where?"

"Don't ask me no questions, Sarge. Then ye can't answer none. But ye might like to know, jest as a bit a news, there's a shed over to the supply depot mighty flimsy put together."

"Right. Come along and meet the others. Mess time."

He was turning to lead the way when the voice caught him, still low, matter of fact. "Easy, Sarge. If it don't rub ye wrong, I'll interduce meself. Might be better that way."

He stepped aside and the big figure moved past carrying its load with casual deceptive ease, and he followed and stopped, back some, watching, and saw the man approach the fire and take a stand at the edge of the flickering light, looking down, and the others shift a bit, uneasy and curious, looking up.

"Evenin', boys." The slight nasal quality, the slight drawl, were a slight edge more apparent. "Zattig's me name. Oncet a sergeant the 14th Indianny. Jest a noncom. The major says ye were all rankers. But I'm bigger'n any a ye an' I reckon that evens it a bit. No need to pass out yer handles, I'll get onto 'em soon enough. I brung us somethin' here to play soldier with."

The silence was there again and he listened, intent, ready to step forward, and he heard Private Webb's voice, mildly superior, patronizing. "Good man. What kind of rifles are those?"

"Springfields, me little man. Springfields. Ye think I'd bother with them heavy Enfields?" The big figure swung sideways and laid the rifles down and slid the string of cartridge boxes beside them and straightened again. "I been earnin' me rations too. What's fir mess?"

"Hardtack," said Private Merriam. "Salt horse an' coffee."

"A sergeant," said Private Stewart Kinsey, softly, gently mocking. "The uncouth bumptious variety. And he doesn't know that."

"I reckon," said Private Zattig, unmoved, undisturbed. "I've et more a the same'n any a one a ye. I was thinkin' mebbe one a ye'd had the sense to snaffle a couple a reb chickens that couldn't take the oath proper."

"Too damn dumb," said Private Geary, irritation roughening his voice. "All of us. And all we have is two tin cups and two tin plates. We'll have to eat in shifts. Merriam there had more and let them be grabbed."

"What would you expect, Geary?" Private Kinsey spoke softly

again, gently mocking again. "A youngster who couldn't even wound himself right."

He saw the stocky, young figure by the fire step back, the heat flush on the face deepening, the hands, hanging limp, clenching tight now, and he was moving forward when the slow, nasal drawl stopped him. "Plain it is, me boys, ye're a bunch a rankers. Used to havin' things served pretty. Ain't that a couple a canteens there? I'll show ye somethin'."

Huge and shambling at the shimmering edge of the firelight, big hands surprisingly deft and sure, Private Zattig scooped up a canteen and unscrewed the cap and shook it to make certain it was empty and ripped away the cloth covering and set it upright on the ground and took a cartridge from one of the belt boxes and ripped it open with his teeth and poured the powder into the canteen. The big hands reached with two small twigs, using them as pincers, and took a tiny ember from the fire and held this at arm's length and dropped it in on the powder. There was a small snuffled explosion and the canteen burst apart at the side seams into two neat halves.

"Well I'll be damned," said Private Owen Selous. "So that's why the things are always disappearing."

"There's a couple a plates," said Private Zattig. "All right, me boy—Merriam ain't it?—ye try now with that other one."

He waited until he heard the small second explosion and then came forward. "Serve up any time you're ready, Merriam. I'll be back in a little while . . ."

The dusk was merging into dark as he left the lane and cut across a long field, swinging past a row of massed artillery batteries parked for the night, toward the few scattered buildings of the crossroads settlement. Light shone through the two side windows of the little two-room shanty as he drew near, angling in from the rear, and he stepped around the corner to the front and stopped short, caught in the blankness of sudden shock. The door was open, light striking out through on a wagon drawn up close, and men moved in and out carrying boxes and small crates and loading them into the wagon.

A man moved out of the darkness close to the wall, into the light, and he recognized one of the clerks.

"Heath?"

"Yes."

"Took your time coming, didn't you. Major Foster says to tell you we're moving a few miles down the line. No need for you to follow. So he says, anyway. For the next few days you can bring any report you have here, same time, and I'll pick it up. Do you have anything now?"

He stared at the other a moment. "Tell him all the men have come in . . . and . . . and we're making out."

"That's simple enough. Try and get here a little earlier next time." The other was moving away and he stood, still and quiet, tasting the added loneliness that even this, some slight contact with a slim, ironic man in a major's uniform, should be cut off, and the other was turning back, taking something from a pocket, another envelope, sealed, and handing it to him.

Slowly he moved around the corner of the shanty to the patch of light from one of the windows. He broke the seal and took out the single, small piece of paper. One line only in neat, precise script: *Carry on, Heath. That is an order.*

Coming back along the lane in the darkness he could see the small upward glow of the fire in the woodlot. Closer and he could begin to see the humped, dark shapes around it. Closer, swinging in over the lone rail, moving quietly, and he slowed, sensing the silence hanging over them. He felt tired, worn by the long day's stretches of waiting and wondering, of constant alertness to the currents between them, of readiness to step in and divert the immediate moment. Closer, and he stopped, listening. It was not a silence. It was a quietness, filled with the barely perceptible small sounds of shifting movements and scrapings. They were eating, using short pieces of sapling whittled flat on the ends for spoons, all of them except Private Fulton, a still, humped shape as he had been before, simply a shell of a man squatted back from the others, staring into the fire.

He heard the voice of Private Selous in the quietness, bluff, hearty, no trace of self-conscious pressure in it. "Just because you found that pot, Geary, doesn't mean you can hog the coffee. It's my turn on that cup."

He straightened in the darkness and stepped forward.

"Back again, sir," said Private Merriam, rising to tip the old bucket and scrape chunks of meat from it onto the canteen-plate he had been using and handing this to him together with a fresh-whittled, little stick. "There's more'n enough. Fulton there claims he ain't hungry. We been savin' this for you."

And a little later. He set his empty plate aside and was aware of Merriam beside him taking it and stacking it on the others and of the other men watching him, waiting, all except Fulton, apart in his own dark shadow, and he took the piece of paper with its single line of script from his jacket pocket and folded it over on one knee, once, twice, and again, and pressed down the folds and spread out the paper open again and tore it carefully along the folds and held in his hands eight tiny, squared scraps of paper. He looked up. "Has anyone a pencil? Anything to write with?"

"Ha!" Private Joseph Webb fumbled in his own jacket pocket and extracted a short chunk of slate pencil and tossed it to him. "That offsets your damn coffeepot, Geary."

He bent forward and began to write on the tiny scraps of paper, a single number on each.

You don't really mean, do you, Sergeant," said Private Kinsey, aloof, gently mocking, "that we're going to play parlor games?"

He looked up again, quiet, steady. "Just drawing for tent mates, Kinsey. Corresponding numbers match up." He folded each small scrap over once and took off his forage cap and dropped them into it and reached to hand it to the man. "We'll give you the honor of first draw . . ."

Small seemingly inconsequential things, chances, happenings, sliding past in their own immediate moments, yet leading to so much, meaning so much, in the long-drawn accumulation of those moments. Small things, like the drawing of tiny scraps of paper out of a dusty, dirtied forage cap. Owen Selous with Joseph Webb. Silas Geary with Hugo Zattig. Jared Heath with Alfred Merriam. And Stewart Kinsey with James Fulton.

And a little later again. He caught himself slipping away in his mind, away from the job that was his to do, that he had been ordered to do, and he pulled his thoughts back from the edge of the slope that ran down to the Spotsylvania road and was aware again of the others watching him, waiting, and he spoke again. "We don't have a bugle. That's probably a good thing. Too loud. I don't think we want to call any particular attention to ourselves. But we need something to take its place."

A slow drawl came from the big figure stretched flat, head cradled on hands folded up under it, feet extended to the fire. "Mebbe one a us can whistle the calls."

He looked around at the others. There was no response. But Private Geary was struggling to extract something from a pants pocket, was speaking, tone touched with belligerence. "Anyone laughs I'll bust him one. But I found this too." Out came the hand and in it was a small mouth organ.

Private Geary sighed, no belligerence in his tone now. "But I can't play the damn thing."

"Fulton can." Private Webb was proud of his information. "I've heard him back in the regiment. Plays one of those things like a goddamned tooting fool."

Private Fulton shrank farther into shadow, head down, voice hoarse, little more than a croak in constricted throat. "I threw it away."

He reached and took the small, tarnished instrument from Geary's outstretched hand and tossed it, falling between Fulton's hunched knees. "But we have one now, Fulton. Try it."

The man's head rose and for an instant the eyes met his, reflecting the firelight, unreadable, and they flicked aside and the head dropped again. But one hand, slow and hesitant, was fumbling between the hunched knees.

"Come on, Fulton," said Private Webb. "Give us that tune you used to back in camp. You know, that Bacchus' sons thing."

Slowly the hand rose from between the knees, wiping back and forth on the cloth of the pants leg, and on up to the lowered head. A few soft tones, feeble, experimental. Then the man had it, the high F, and held it, strengthening, and dropped into the downward sweep of "Garryowen" . . .

"Out a the mouth a babes," came the low voice of Private Zattig. "I'd give me right arm to have the gift a that. Fulton, me boy, do ye know the Wabash one?"

He pulled himself again into the passing moment, the

immediate necessity. "Not now, Zattig. There'll be times enough to wear him and that harmonica out." He turned toward Fulton, crisp, incisive, catching at the brief upsurge of spirit in the man. "All right. Let's see what you can do. Give me assembly."

Again the eyes met his and held now, bright in the flickering firelight, revealing nothing. But the hands with the small bit of wood and metal between them were rising. Clear and clean it came, the staccato summoning call.

"Good. Now drill." And again it came, the quickening pulsing beat.

He rose to his feet. "That does it, Fulton. You're it. Bugler, band, the whole works. A trifle tough on you because you'll have to be the first up. But that will excuse you from your turn as cook. Reveille in the morning a half-hour after sunrise . . . Now, ten minutes while we wrassle with Kinsey's blankets, then you can give us taps . . ."

He stood by the fading fire and with one heavy shoe scraped the embers inward to a small pile. He moved away into the darkness and to the first of the low patched tents along the level stretch by the fence and stooped to peer in. Vaguely he could distinguish the dark shape of Merriam wrapped in a blanket along the right side. He reached and felt for his own that he had laid folded just inside to the left, and his fingers rubbed over it, finding it unfolded, spread out for him. He sat on the ground and took off his heavy shoes and reached to set them inside close to the canvas where it was pegged down. He sat there quiet, waiting, and the first notes came from down the line, past the last tent, soft and clear, trembling along the night air, serene and haunting in the darkness of the night. They wavered and came again, through to the finish, floating off through the trees of the woodlot and sinking into silence.

He listened. There was no sound, none whatever, down by the last tent. He rose and moved quietly around and along between the closed-off backs of the tents and the fence, peering into the darkness. Ahead, past the last tent, turned away, he saw the hunched shape on the ground, a blacker outline in the night. He eased closer and sensed rather than saw the shaking of the shoulders and heard the faint gasps of the choked-down, sobbing breaths.

He was suddenly old and tired and an angry irritation grated in him that he should be drawn from his own quest for certainty within himself to play nursemaid to the softnesses and weaknesses of other men, and deliberately he pushed this aside and his muscles were gathering to move forward when he heard another sound, a footfall from near the last tent. Another shape was approaching, unrecognizable in the darkness. Quiet, motionless, unseen, he heard the low whisper, the voice of Private Stewart Kinsey, not mocking, low and roughened. "Quit it, kid. Nothing's ever that bad. Come along. It's damned lonesome in that tent alone . . ."

And later, perhaps a long while later. He lay wrapped in his blanket, head pillowed on one of the knapsacks found laid-ready for him, sleepless, unable to sleep, thoughts ranging far from a small woodlot and the problems concentrated there, when his whole body tensed in sudden awareness of movement a few feet away under the low canvas. Private Merriam was stirring, folding aside his blanket and inching slowly, cautiously, off it and out of the tent. He lay still, careful to keep his breath even, regular, and the other inched on, on out, and sat up fumbling to pull on shoes and rose and he could hear the soft steps away.

He pushed up on one elbow, straining to catch the direction, and suddenly he heard what the younger ears, alert to it, had heard before him, the dim, muffled, far-off, ragged cadence of tired replacement troops in night march along the distant road.

He lay back and time passed and he lay there sleepless, unable to sleep, his thoughts pegged by some obscure sense of obligation to the problems concentrated in a small woodlot, and he knew without confronting the knowing that somehow this waiting, now, this night, was a test that would fasten that sense of obligation upon him or release him from it, and time passed, much or little he could not know, and suddenly his body tensed again in awareness of movement outside.

He heard the soft, small sounds of articles being lowered cautiously to the ground. He heard the soft stirrings of a stocky, young body inching in over the blanket a few feet away under the low canvas and before they had ceased his tired muscles had relaxed and sleep had claimed him.

And in the morning. He was coming back from a quick scrubbing in the little stream that cut through the farthest corner of the woodlot, pulling on his jacket, when he heard the shout, high, angry, and saw ahead Private Webb standing in the lane, just outside the entrance break, and the others hurrying there. He quickened his own stride and pushed in among them, gathered now in taut semicircle around the old board he had fastened to the top rail.

"Look at that sign, Heath!" Private Webb's voice shook with fury. "I told you I didn't like this business! Do we have to stand for things like that?"

The old board hung along the rail as he had fastened it. The letters he had marked were as he had made them: COMPANY Q. And beneath, scratched into the old wood by nail point or knife, were more letters: CAMP COWARDICE.

He felt them looking at him, staring at him, all but one and that one, broad, stubble-bearded face set in stubborn anger, power in him no longer slack but driving into long purposeful strides, was moving away along the lane, and he turned, facing after the man, and his own voice reached out, instinctive, like a whip snapping. "Zattig!"

The big man hesitated, stopped, swung around, a hard glaze over the eyes in the broad angry face. "The low-livin' bastard can't be far! I'll learn 'im something!"

For an instant the others were unimportant, were not there. This was between the two of them. He spoke again, quiet, steady. "That won't wipe away the name, Zattig. You will stay here."

He saw the hard glaze fading from the man's eyes, not the acceptance of what he had said but of the fact that he had said it, and the tension easing out of the long, taut muscles, and he turned back to the others.

"Well, Heath." Private Webb, still furious, made himself the spokesman. "You're supposed to be the officer here. What are you going to do about it?"

Do about it? The question struck him with a dry humorless ironic amusement. Let it stand. What difference did it make? But they were looking at him, staring at him, an angry uneasiness on them.

"Merriam. Get me the ax."

He hefted it, measuring the stroke, and swung and the blade bit into the old wood and the lower half of the board with the lower line of scratched letters dropped to the ground. He leaned over and picked it up and handed it to Private Webb. "Tuck that away somewhere. It'll make a good target for rifle practice this afternoon . . ."

And later that morning. They had gathered on the level stretch in front of the tents at the call to drill. Rifles and cartridge boxes and what else they had, with Private Merriam's midnight additions, had been distributed. There had been some joking at themselves as they assembled, at their mismatched, motley, orphaned array, and this had dwindled and they stood in a silence whose weight over them steadily increased. He had them lined up, dressed to the right, according to the school of the company hammered into him in the first weeks of his enlistment, by height from right to left: Zattig, Kinsey, Webb, Geary, Fulton, Selous, Merriam. He stood in front, facing them, aware that all this too was ridiculous, seen from without a caricature of military procedure, and yet, seen from within, felt, understood, something that had to be done, that he must find a way to do, and he moved to take his position by rank at the left end of the line, his mind pushing at the problem of adapting company commands and movements to a single small squad.

It was the voice of Private Geary that stopped him in stride. "Good God, man! Are you really going ahead with this?"

He was conscious of the edge, the beginning of anger creeping into his own voice. "Put your remark properly, Mr. Geary." That was wrong, jangling, off-key, but it was said.

Private Geary looked at him, deliberately delaying, eyes narrowing. The one word, when it came, was denied by the tone. "Sir."

"The answer, Mr. Geary, is yes."

"Oh, come now, Sergeant," said Private Kinsey, soft-voiced, gently mocking. "Are you sure you're not just interested in strutting authority?"

He felt the anger rising in him and with it a desire to let it rise, to let it break into action, and it hit against the hard base of his being now and he knew that it was an anger, not at these men and their words but at himself and the impossible, ridiculous difficulties confronting him, and at the knowing it faded with a finality that would he forever and he spoke again, quiet, steady. "Kinsey . . . Geary . . . as long as I am in command of this company we will drill. If we are going to have any trouble about it, let's have it now."

He waited, wondering which would be the one to make the move whatever it would be.

"Christ almighty, Heath!" said Private Geary. "Can't you see how silly—"

"Shut up, Geary!" Private Kinsey's voice had a sudden keenness, a suggestion of a knife edge in the man. "You're just yapping trying to show yourself you amount to something! Maybe we all are!" The voice changed, flat, impersonal. "Heath. We all know you don't have any real authority. Nothing to back you up. But we all know too that if anyone raises a ruckus this whole cock-eyed Company Q business falls apart. It probably will anyway. But there's no sense deliberately doing it." Private Kinsey sighed, voice changing again, soft again, touched with a trace of the mockery perhaps not so much meant as simply habitual. "Ah, well, Sergeant . . . If you're going to do it, go ahead, push the farce along."

He nodded, seeing this clear now, and turned slightly, toward the right end of the line. "Zattig! Five paces . . . forward!"

The big man, watching him intently, broad face stolid, unreadable, stepped forward.

"About . . . face!"

The big man swung smartly around, facing the others now.

"All right, Zattig. You know more about this than I do. Than any of the rest of us. Take over."

Slowly, deliberately, he strode to the line of men, estimating his own height against them, and pushed in between Webb and Geary, and turned about.

He saw the slow smile spreading on the broad, flat face and

behind it something more, a groping after some thought, some emotion, perhaps never before quite grasped. The man's smile dwindled and was gone.

"It's the kind a thing," said Private Zattig, "that oughta make a old-line sarge like me kick up me heels. A chancet to make a bunch a rankers sweat." One big hand rose and rubbed along the back of his neck, hard, and rubbed down along under the chin. "Only some-such way I don't feel—"

Private Zattig stopped speaking, head turning toward the sound of voices over by the break in the rail fence. Two men were there, in the lane, staring at the remaining half of the old board, pointing it out to each other. They wore clean, neat uniforms with the scarlet edging of the artillery. They looked out over the wood-lot, finding obvious amusement at what they saw.

"Take a good look," said one to the other, deliberately raising his voice. "It ain't every day you can see a batch of yellowbellies trying to act like soldiers."

Private Zattig's head turned back. "Stay right here, me boys. This is me own meat." And he was moving toward the rail fence, wide, sloping shoulders swinging, power driving into long, loose-jointed strides, and Sergeant Jared Heath stood in line with the others, rigid, watching, waiting, holding to the single fact caught as the man swung away, that there was no hard glaze over the eyes in the stubborn, chipped, stone set of the face.

The two men in the lane, silent now, stared at the big figure approaching. It halted at the fence, just behind the old board hanging by the rusty wire, and set its rifle against the fence and leaned forward, two big hands gripping the top rail.

"A fine mornin'," said Private Zattig, definitely drawling, cheer-ful, somehow chilling in his very cheerfulness. "Or it was till the artill'ry took to cloudin' it some. Anybody says anything about me squad says it to me." The broad face sighted straight at the man who had spoken. "Ye sayin' anythin'?"

The man was a statue, motionless, apparently unable to move. "Aw, come along, Joe," said his companion, edging away. "We're late already."

Private Zattig watched the two of them start away along the lane. One big hand scooped up the rifle and the big figure swung around and strode back to take its stand facing the line.

"Good man," said Private Webb. "You handled that like—"

"Ye'll shut yer yap, Mr. Webb," said Private Zattig, serene, matter of fact. "An' I've made up me mind. All a us ran out before some-such way or other. We ain't runnin' out now. We're doin' what the sarge says. We're drillin'. . . Ten . . . shun! Right . . . dress!"

Slowly, big head shaking in disgust, Private Zattig ambled to position at the left end of the line, looking down along it. His voice dropped to a low rumble in his throat. "Did anybody ever snaffle a worse bunch a misfits to try to make into men." His voice rose in a rough, heartwarming roar. "Selous! Suck in that belly! It's stickin' out like a woman with twins . . . Heath! Take holt a that gun like ye know what it's for! It ain't rabbits ye'll be usin' it on . . . Eyes . . . front! Shoulder . . . arms! Mark yer numbers now! In two ranks, form company . . . march!"

Ragged, bumping into one another as the odd numbers moved ahead and the even swung in behind, Company Q stepped forward . . .

And that afternoon. He sat cross-legged in front of the first tent with several folded-over blank pages from the small, leather-laced account book in one hand, the short piece of slate pencil in the other, marking in headings for an improvised company book. A few feet away Private Merriam sat hunched over, right leg out straight, left leg doubled up, shoe off, gently massaging the foot. A little farther away, in front of their own tent, Privates Selous and Webb squatted by a squared-off chunk of old board dotted with light and dark pebbles, playing checkers. Over by the remains of the fire Private Geary, sour-faced, sullen, was unpacking rations from a burlap bag. Beyond, Private Zattig stooped to dump a huge armload of deadwood, culled from the woodlot, at the feet of Private Fulton, who stood waiting, leaning on the ax.

He looked up at the sound of voices, faint, indistinguishable, from the farthest corner of the woodlot where the small stream cut through. He listened and heard, faint but clear, anger riding it, the voice of Private Kinsey. "Say that again, you filthy-mouthed fool, and I'll show you who's a coward!"

Another voice, low, indistinct, then the sound of thrashing activity in the far brush.

He was up, running, conscious that the others were moving too, and he broke through bushes and saw, on the near edge of the stream, Private Kinsey, cap gone, hair flying, handsome face flushed and already battered, mixing furiously with two strangers in cavalry uniforms. He caught a glimpse of two horses a short distance down the stream, heads low, drinking in routine indifference to the scrambling melee above them, then his attention was concentrated on the others around him, on Fulton, white-faced, staring, and Geary, still sour-faced, contemptuous, and Selous and Webb just puffing up, all these to his right, and to the left Zattig, striding forward, the light of battle leaping on broad face, and Merriam, tagging, trying to keep up, hopping, limping on shoeless left foot.

"Zattig! Merriam! Hold it!"

He watched the unequal struggle twenty feet away at the edge of the stream. Private Kinsey was definitely taking a beating. Deliberately he turned toward the right. "Fulton!"

The man's eyes shifted to him and he spoke again. "There's two of them."

He saw understanding creep into the man's eyes, wide, staring at him, followed by a fear, not perhaps of anything physical but of the psychic necessity to decide, to drive himself into doing, into moving, and the eyes pulled away from him, staring now at Kinsey and the two men hammering him between them.

Slowly, reluctantly, Private Fulton took a step forward. And another. And suddenly, frantic, desperate, breath sobbing in his throat, Private Fulton was driving headlong into one of the cavalrymen . . .

And perhaps fifteen minutes later. He sat again in front of the first tent, improvised company book on one knee, looking up. Privates Kinsey and Fulton stood facing him, marks of a thorough licking apparent on both. Off to the side were the others, watching, listening.

"Leave Fulton out of this," said Private Kinsey. "I'm the one started it."

"Right. Fulton simply obeyed orders. What do you think I ought to do with you, Kinsey?"

"Slap me with mess duty for a while, I suppose. Something like that," said Private Kinsey cheerfully, a trace of mockery that meant nothing in his voice. "Go ahead, Heath, think up another nasty one. It was worth it . . ."

And in the morning, early. He slept, the first deep sleep of weeks, lost in it, unaware of footsteps and voices outside by the other tents, of Private Merriam sitting up and crawling out of their own tent. It was Merriam who, a few moments later, peered in, calling him.

He came awake, fighting up out of the sleep, and tried to rise to his feet and bumped his head on the low ridgepole and ducked down, scrambling out.

"It's Geary, sir! He's gone!"

He stood erect. In the dim light of dawn filtering through the trees of the woodlot he could see Private Merriam staring at him. He strode to the next tent and looked in. It was empty.

"Where's Zattig?"

"Gone chasin' him, sir."

Two more shapes, blurred in the half-light, were there. Webb. Fulton.

"And Kinsey?"

"After him too. Anyways he went chasin' along after Zattig."

He looked on down by the other tents. There was no one else. "How about Selous?"

"Took out too," said Private Webb. "I tried to stop him, a man his age chasing around the countryside this time of morning. But he went anyway."

"With them?"

"Well, he was trying to keep up with Kinsey."

He turned away and went back to the first tent and pulled out his shoes and sat on the ground to put these on. He sat there, still and quiet. The others, confused, aimless, gathered near.

"Well, Heath," said Private Webb. "What are we going to do?"

"We're going to wait, Webb . . . You might stir up a fire. And make a pot of coffee."

He reached behind him and took hold of his blanket and pulled it out and up around his shoulders and for a while he watched the others near the growing fire and time passed and he forgot them and the light increased, the sun rising and fighting through a rim of clouds, and Private Merriam brought him coffee and he took this mechanically and drank it and set the tin cup aside and sat there, still and quiet, the blanket up around him, and at last he saw the far figures, caught in glimpses through the trees of the woodlot, coming across the wide field beyond. Three of them. No. Four. One lagging well behind.

They came closer, moving through the trees, into the cleared corner that was the camp, Private Geary in front, dirty, disheveled, dark bruises discoloring one cheek, head high, defiance and deep bitter anger plain on his face, Privates Zattig and Kinsey close behind, determined, contemptuous, and farther back Private Selous, winded, puffing, square-cut beard bobbing in the effort of hurrying to catch up.

They stood facing him. He pushed the blanket off his shoulders and put his arms back, hands flat, leaning against the firmness of the ground and the hard rock of resolution within him. Deliberately he ignored Geary. "Zattig! Speak up! What do you have to say for yourself?"

"What do ye mean, Sarge?" The big man was baffled, bewildered.

"Why did you go after him?"

"He was runnin' out, Sarge. Desertin'."

"You are responsible for yourself here, Zattig. Not for anyone else . . . Kinsey! How about you?"

The eyes were narrowing in the battered, handsome face. The voice was soft, mocking, "I figured that if the rest of us can take it, he can too."

"That is for him to decide, Kinsey. Not you . . . Selous?"

"Good God, Heath! You're off on a tangent!" Private Selous was red-faced, indignant. "We begin to get us a little something here a man can hold on to and this stiff-necked turncoat who can't face up to things tries to break it. You think I'd—"

"It's no good, Selous. Not if it can be broken that easily." He looked straight at Geary. "You will have to forget what they did to you, Geary. They didn't know . . . You can go again now and no one will stop you. And no report will be made until the usual time tonight."

He could feel the puzzled, angry defiance of the man beating at him. "You're a sniveling, sentimental coward, Heath! You really mean that, don't you?"

"Yes."

He saw the slender, erect figure swing around and start away, striding again toward the wide field beyond, taking away whatever had been wrought in that woodlot in the last two days and whatever chance he would have to do what he had been ordered to do, and he sat there, still and quiet, leaning back, and he saw the man slow, and stop, and stand motionless, head up, and turn and come back, straight to him.

"God damn you to eternal hell, Heath!" said Private Geary, fury twisting his lean, fine-featured face, and strode on to the second tent and dropped to crawl inside and lie flat on his blanket, face down and turned toward the blank canvas wall.

He rose to his feet to start the day, holding within, clinched into mind forever, the memory of a taut, tormented man thanking him with a curse on a cloudy morning in a small, isolated woodlot in northern Virginia . . .

And that evening. There was no uniformed clerk to meet him at the little two-room shanty. It was a supply warehouse now, dark and forlorn at the moment, a padlock on the door. Wagons rumbled past on the road in the almost endless procession toward the battlefront sidling ever farther off southeastward. Across the way glimmered the innumerable small fires of several raw, new regiments in night bivouac. He stood in the deep, dark of the shanty shadow and waited and no one came and he moved away, walking slowly back the way he had come.

From along the lane he could see the glow of their fire, hear the soft tones of a mouth organ as Private Fulton wove casual, intricate frills in and around the familiar strains of "Swanee River," and he knew that Private Zattig would be stretched flat, hands clasped under big head, humming a low, tone-deaf, tuneless accompaniment.

He moved in through the entrance break and approached the fire and took a place among them and the tin plate heaped with food and the tin cup of coffee handed him by Private Kinsey.

He raised his head higher. A horse was coming along the lane, not fast, jogging in slow tired rhythm. It passed the entrance break, and stopped, and turned back, walking now, and picked its way through and came toward the fire, and stopped again, and he could see in the reaching, flickering, light the slender, neat figure, worn and weary in the saddle. He started to rise and the others were stirring too.

"At ease, gentlemen," said Major Foster, swinging down. "Perhaps you could feed a hungry man who hasn't had time to stop for a meal since breakfast . . ."

Major Foster sat between Privates Selous and Webb, balancing a full plate on one knee, holding a fork in the other hand. "I see rifles racked over there. And tents. I have here a plate, well filled. And a fork. Your sergeant's brief, very noncommittal reports must be correct. You are making out."

Major Foster speared a chunk of meat and put it in his mouth. A tired, grim smile touched his face. "This is not salt pork."

"That's fresh, sir," said Private Selous, a note of pride in his voice. "Damn near too fresh. Merriam here came across a rebel pig that wouldn't stop when challenged."

"And who butchered it?"

"Geary."

Major Foster's eyebrows rose a bit. "And who cooked this?"

"Kinsey."

Major Foster's eyebrows rose higher. He nodded slowly and bent to his meal . . .

Major Foster laid his plate carefully on the ground and set his emptied cup upon it. Partway around the fire the big shape of Private Zattig rose from propped elbows to sitting position. "You want, Major, to talk to the sarge alone?"

"No," said Major Foster. "I want to talk to all of you . . . And what you appear to have managed to accomplish here makes that difficult . . . I came here tonight to confess failure. I started this and I have been unable to carry it through. I have found no regiment that will accept you . . ."

It was Private Kinsey who spoke, from the shadow beyond Private Zattig, where he was quietly stacking plates and cups. "You must have some pull, Major, or you couldn't have started it. Just get the department to ram us down some colonel's throat. We can take it."

"Nothing is ever that simple, Kinsey," said Major Foster. "I have been bound from the beginning by the stipulation that you must be voluntarily accepted. Perhaps I overestimated my powers of persuasion. The plain fact seems to be that no one wants you. No, that is not quite correct. I have by no means covered the entire corps. But the matter has been taken out of my hands. This morning I received orders to disband Company Q. The reason cited: the war is in a critical stage and the Army of the Potomac has no time for experiments . . ."

"Christ amighty!" said Private Geary, anger flaring in his voice. "Then why the hell are you sitting here jabbering like an old maid?"

Major Foster straightened, raising his head higher. "Because, Mr. Geary, I do happen to have, in some slight measure, what Mr. Kinsey refers to as pull. I have been on the wire to Washington and I have perhaps salvaged something. Perhaps not. But I felt that, having brought you all together, I was under some obligation to try to give you a chance to stay together. As a unit. Under your own officer."

Major Foster pulled an envelope from a coat pocket and tapped it gently against one knee. "This is the situation. The War Department is scraping up men now from wherever possible. It regards you, all those like you, as of value only to relieve other men from routine duties for battle service. I have here orders for you, authorized from Washington, sending you, as a unit, as replacements to one of the western frontier posts that has been stripped of most of its regular garrison for duty here with the army in Virginia. That is not what I had in mind at the start, not what I promised you. But it is the best I can do now. And it would keep you together . . . On the other hand, if you prefer, I will toss this envelope into this fire. Company Q will be disbanded and you will return, as individuals, to your previous scattered assignments under the quartermaster. The choice is yours . . ."

He leaned back, hands flat against the firmness of the earth, and the thought hit him, *Now it breaks, this too, and always and forever everything will break,* and he leaned back, waiting, and he was aware of a silence around the fire, of restless stirrings and shiftings of position, and over all of a silence when there should have been voices breaking it, and then there was a voice, low and rumbling in a big throat.

"Ye give us a man, Major," said Private Zattig. "We been gettin' along. Doin' what he says."

Major Foster looked across the fire at him. "Well, Heath?"

It came unbidden, instinctive, out of whatever the long-hammering of circumstance had made him now. "We'll stay together."

He stood in the darkness by the break in the rail fence, an unopened envelope in his hand, and the horse was simply a blacker shadow a few feet away, and the slender man swinging up to the saddle. He had the feeling that there were innumerable things that he ought to be saying, that he wanted to be saying, and there was nothing, nothing that he could put into words.

Major Foster sighed, an audible sound in the darkness, and weariness showed in his voice. "The whole war seems to be getting out of hand, Heath. Overwhelming everything decent a man might try to do. Perhaps you are better out of it." The voice steadied and the familiar cool, impersonal irony of tone dropped down to him. "Foster's Foolishness was a prophetic title. It was a mistake, yes. But it was not one of intention. Think what you will of me hereafter, Heath. But remember that."

He listened to the hoofbeats dying away into distance and turned and walked slowly back to the dwindling fire and the figures around it.

"We're only human, man," said Private Selous, bluff, hearty. "What the devil's in that envelope?"

He opened it and took out the single sheet of paper and knelt by the fire to read aloud.

Sergeant Jared Heath:
This will confirm your appointment, first sergeant, Company Q,

detached special service under the Judge Advocate General's office. You will at once draw strictly necessary funds, as computed by him, from the Deputy Paymaster General, and conduct your company by the most direct route to Fort Leavenworth, Kansas, thence by whatever means practicable to Fort Union, New Mexico Territory, placing yourself and company upon arrival under the orders of Major James Pattison.

MAJOR MATTHEW FOSTER
Judge Advocate, 2nd Corps

Five

There is a gap now of two months and three weeks, shade it a few days either way, and of two thousand miles more or less, probably more if the route were stretched out straight. That in itself, perhaps, if the facts could be known, would be a full story, the long journey of eight men, of seven other men and Jared Heath, from a small woodlot near Spotsylvania Court House in old Virginia to Fort Union in that portion of even older Mexico that had become New Mexico Territory.

Not just eight men. A company. A queer, crippled, motley, orphaned or rather parentless fragment of a caricature of a company, insignia-less, tossed aside, unwanted, a tight little unit drawn together in a shared, stubborn and somehow defiant indifference to circumstance and the world about, led by a solid, compact, square-shouldered man with improvised stripes of a sergeant on the sleeves of an ill-fitting jacket, encountering questions and quips and difficulties and disbelief and delays everywhere along the way.

And yet the man himself, in the later years, looking back, summed it in two short sentences:

"We were ordered to Fort Union. So we went there."

Not the old Fort Union far to the north on the Big Muddy, the Missouri, about where the Montana-North Dakota line is today, famous in the early fur trade. The new Fort Union, far to the south in eastern New Mexico, in the valley of the Mora River a few miles above the present little village of Watrous, close to the junction of the two branches of the old Santa Fe Trail southwestward out of Westport, now Kansas City, that merged again here for the last long stretch through Glorietta Pass and Apache Canyon on to the old Spanish provincial capital. Colonel E. V. Sumner had chosen the site on the west side of Coyote Creek and ordered up the first log buildings in 1851, one of his first moves as new commander of troops in this territory acquired in the recent Mexican War. He was a strict disciplinarian, this Colonel Sumner, and he had a double purpose, to establish a military supply depot for the southwestern army posts and to remove his headquarters troops from the temptations and dissipations of what he described as "that sink of vice and extravagance" and was really only easygoing, leisurely, fandangoing Santa Fe. He removed them all right, about one hundred miles eastward, around and past the lower end of that great mountain range extending down from Colorado known as the Sangre de Cristo, out on the beginnings of the seemingly limitless vegas, plains, lying between long ridges of rock, that gave the name to the town of Las Vegas and ran on then as they run on now to merge into the storied Llano Estacado of western Texas.

And yet, to be precise, to nail it down as historians do, not even that Fort Union, not Colonel Sumner's Fort Union. The even newer Fort Union, Colonel L. R. Canby's, across the creek from Colonel Sumner's, begun in 1861 when Colonel Canby was commander of Union troops in the Territory.

Those were hectic days in the southwestern territories, ripped by repercussions of the Civil War breaking into action along the far eastern seaboard. Officer after officer, almost a majority of the trained men, the West Pointers, were resigning, slipping away to join the Confederate cause. Many of them would write their names large into history in the east, men like William James Longstreet, a colonel then, serving as paymaster for the territories of New Mexico and Arizona, who handed in a careful record of his accounts and departed to become the hard-hitting right hand of Robert L. Lee. And another of them, another colonel, Henry Hopkins Sibley, had left for Texas and was there, in Texas, in mid-1861, recruiting a force for an invasion up through New Mexico to take over the rich mines of Colorado to help finance the new Confederacy. Only Fort Union and its few satellite posts down along the Rio Grande Valley stood in the path of such an invasion—and this Fort Union, Colonel Sumner's, stood in all unfavorable defensive position, close to a long commanding ridge from which offensive fire could be poured almost directly down into it.

Colonel Canby hurriedly corrected that mistake, in part at least, though it was fortunate that the fighting never reached the Mora valley because his site too would still have been within range of cannon shot from the ridge. About a mile eastward, across the creek, he built a large, star-shaped earthwork redoubt complete with ditches, parapets, and bombproof shelters. Here he would make his stand in extremity. And Sibley's invasion, along in 1862, became a reality and the Confederate invaders moved up the Rio Grande, driving the Union forces into constant retreat, defeating them again and again, taking over Albuquerque and Santa Fe itself, moving out eastward from there to threaten Fort Union. And down from Colorado came a regiment of volunteers and with other Union troops that had gathered at the fort marched westward to meet the invaders and in Glorietta Pass, in one of the most ironic clashes on record, the invaders clearly won the battle in the field and the Union troops as clearly won the campaign by stumbling upon and destroying the Confederate wagon train. Short now on food and ammunition and pack animals, in a semi-arid land where foraging was wasted effort, the invaders began the long withdrawal back to Texas. And Colonel Canby, with the war pressure dwindling away, turned among other things to the building of his Fort Union, begun with his earthwork redoubt on the east side of Coyote Creek.

Now, in the summer of 1864, all that was over and done and the Civil War as such, though rising toward its long final climax in the East, was far from New Mexico, touching the territory only indirectly through supply shortages and the removal of regular troops that thinned down many post garrisons to little more than maintenance squads. That in its turn had brought its own troubles as it encouraged the mountain and the Plains Indians, particularly the Plains Indians, the historic raiders of the region, to increased widespread attacks on wagon trains crossing the lonely stretches and on the few, far-scattered homesteads and ranches and settlements.

Brigadier General J. H. Carleton, who had led several California volunteer regiments eastward in 1862, turning back another Confederate column in Arizona on the way but arriving in New Mexico after the brief war flare there was finished, was now commander of the territory, civil as well as military, ruling under wartime martial law from personal headquarters at Santa Fe, a grim, determined man keeping his California men busy on Indian campaigns, primarily against the Apaches and Navajos of the Rio Grande area and westward, with a ruthlessness that suggested extermination rather than control was his goal.

And there, in eastern New Mexico, well back from the east bank of Coyote Creek in the valley of the Mora, exact site settled now, the sturdy buildings of Fort Union were rising, stone-foundationed, adobe-walled, brick-copinged, flat-roofed, establishing the territorial style of architecture that would spread through the territory and be followed, years later, in the building of the state capitol at Santa Fe.

Getting there from far Virginia would have been problem enough in those days. Wartime conditions must have made it particularly difficult, particularly for men in mismatched, insignia-less uniforms, armed against official curiosity and red tape only with a single, small sheet of paper showing orders in a neat, precise script.

They hiked to Fredericksburg, perhaps picking up wagon rides some of the way, carrying with them all their garnered, improvised equipment with all identifying markings removed or obliterated. From there northward by rail, making whatever connections were possible with hikings between, perhaps up into Pennsylvania, then westward across southern Ohio and Indiana and Illinois into Missouri, on to the railhead at West-port Landing where Kansas City sprawls today. On foot again, they tramped the relatively short distance up the river to Fort Leavenworth. There they lost perhaps a week, confined to an abandoned shed for quarters, while the fort commandant, frankly disbelieving their orders, sent on up the river to the Overland Telegraph office at Council Bluffs and at last, indignant, disgusted, contemptuous, reply from Washington in hand, pushed them on, pressed into service as teamsters with supply wagons heading out westward to Fort Riley. As teamsters they made the long, last overland stretch, with the wagon trains lumbering into the far West, southwestward out of Fort Riley to hit the old Santa Fe Trail at Walnut Creek Ranch on the Arkansas; westward along the river past Fort Larned and the Cimarron Crossing, where Dodge City would rear its wickedness in a few years and where the southern cutoff dropped away down through the dry and dangerous Indian Nations; on along the northern route still following the Arkansas past Bent's New Fort, taken over now by the army, to the crumbling ruins of Bent's Old Fort destroyed in a burst of despair after a cholera epidemic by William Bent himself fifteen years before; southward then in the widening wheel ruts of the worn trail, down through Raton Pass and along close to the foothills of the Sangre de Cristo, into the wide valley of the Mora with the sturdy, brick-capped buildings of Fort Union, some finished now, others still rising, seen far ahead in the clean, eye-stretching distance.

That much is known, pieced together out of meager hints, the route, in general, that they followed, that they had to follow, given the time and the circumstances. That they followed it at all, again given the time and the circumstances and what they themselves were, is remarkable, surprising, against reason and expectation, a strange thin thread of individual shared destinies running through and lost in the turmoil and confusion and whipping-forward currents of the history of a nation in the making in those years. Yet to them, at least to Jared Heath, the one among them whose later, long later, account can be traced, what happened along the way seems to have been unimportant, not worth the remembering or at least the recalling in words. It was to him simply a moving from one place to another, something to be done, and it was done.

"We were ordered to Fort Union. So we went there."

And one other comment, a tribute to a young man who had lost almost all semblance of youth in the twisting strain of his own inner torment:

"We might not have made it without that damned harmonica."

Major James Pattison, captain by permanent rank, major by brevet after the battle of Valverde during Sibley's invasion, present post-transportation officer, sat on an upturned box in the shade of a canvas awning poled out from one of the connected buildings of the mechanics or shops quadrangle, game leg straight in front of him, watching his men, most of them civilians, many of them Spanish-Americans, supposedly wheelwrights, blacksmiths, carpenters, at work on wagon repairs. No doubt his prevailing mood of resigned irritation was upon him, made habitual by a once-wounded, permanently-stiffened leg that kept him from more active duty and the fact that so many of his men, able enough workers when they wanted to be, so rarely saw much sense in any such wanting.

The creaking rumble of heavy wagons long on the road, wheels complaining against greaseless axles, came to him, moving along past the transportation corrals behind the long outside buildings of the quadrangle, out of sight but plainly heard, on swinging in around to the wide space between the big storehouses and the depot office beyond. From the sounds, a considerable train. No doubt Major Pattison sighed, grumbling to himself. Never a train, not one coming down the long trail from the north, not in this deceptively dry climate and this only seemingly level country, without more work being pushed into his already cluttered, crowded quadrangle. Harness worn and a patchwork of hasty on-the-road repairs, axles broken or split, wheels shrunk with metal rims hanging against wrapped-around rope and wire, bed boards warped and sprung. And the paperwork involved, required to satisfy far-off, fussy, office-bound superiors who could not comprehend, who apparently wouldn't even try to comprehend, conditions out here, was an endless, hopeless headache.

Major Pattison looked down at his stiff leg, probably foreseeing new tasks, probably already planning how to meet them. He was a man who grumbled and schemed and grumbled and figured and grumbled and got things done, on time, right. He looked up. His crews were stopping work, were staring at a small tight group of men coming across the quadrangle toward him. Eight of them. Scarecrow burlesques of soldiers in what once might have been uniforms picked at random out of a castaway pile, ill-fitting and worn and patched. All of them had battered-blank knapsacks, each with an old blanket folded and strapped to it. Four of them had ragged rolls of pieced-together canvas bent down over left shoulders, bulging out grotesquely over their knapsacks, ends tied together at right waists. One of them had an old ax strapped with his blanket. Another had an old harness strap wrapped around and around the remnants of his left shoe that gave him a weird, lopsided stride. And all of them carried polished, shining, efficient-looking Springfield rifles.

They stopped, facing him, still in that tight grouping, erect, at attention, tattered, mismatched, assorted scarecrows of soldiers, and one of them stepped a pace forward, a man of medium height, solid, compact, square-shouldered, once seen never to be forgotten, not for anything striking or unusual in size or shape or general appearance but for the feeling of grim controlled resolution that came from him, and for the look in the eyes, clear and clean and cold.

The man spoke, quiet, steady. "Company Q, sir. Reporting for duty as ordered."

"Jesu Becky!" said Major Pattison. "I didn't believe it when I got that crazy letter. I don't believe it now."

Here again, with this Major Pattison as before with Major Foster, it would be interesting to know more of his background. But that again would be to run down a side trail. He is, or rather was, invaluable to this story, not alone for what he did but for the information he provided. He did not understand that information. But he did provide it.

A bachelor, apparently a meticulous correspondent in his meager personal affairs, he wrote a letter once a month during his service at Fort Union, occasionally skipping one and making it up in the next, to a sister back home in Illinois, usually brief, usually merely factual, summing his health and activities and citing any extraordinary events that disturbed his daily routine. These letters seem to have lacked the flavor of his daily speech, but what they lacked in flavor they made up in fact. He kept copies of them in a standard copybook. Perhaps not copies; instead simply items jotted down from day to day or week to week to be polished and amplified and transferred to other paper for the actual letters. But certainly those items preserve the data, the gist, even whole passages of the letters themselves.

For a few years after the war, honorably retired, reasonably comfortable on his pension, perhaps reluctant to return to Illinois with no more glory than action in a single battle of the brief flare of war activity in a far territory, perhaps caught in the curious spell the Southwest imposes on those who will submit to it, having few ties left in Illinois anyway, Major Pattison lived in Santa Fe, a familiar figure on the plaza, moving from one bench to another, both accepted as his, regular as clockwork, to enjoy the clear golden glory, lovelier there than anywhere else, of the morning and the afternoon sun. There, in Santa Fe, in the early seventies, he died of a rheumatic fever probably induced by his wound, probably grumbling and getting the business of dying done with a minimum of trouble for others. And there, years later, many years later, his copybook, together with a few of the published war memoirs he had collected, turned up in an old bookstore—and started the search for the story of a man named Jared Heath.

I wanted to stand up and salute that man. All the way from Virginia with the damndest collection of odd-sized scarecrows you could cull from the whole damned army. And all he said was: "Reporting for duty."

Major Pattison surveyed his new responsibilities. He shuddered visibly at the sight. He started to rise and remembered his leg and thought better of it. He looked down at the leg and began to rub a hand along the thigh, massaging it. "Everything's dumped on me. Why? Isn't there another cracked-up officer in the whole flag-waving, fusspotting army can do a damn thing?" He looked up. "Jesu Becky Maria! I thought you wouldn't get here! Matter of fact, I hoped you wouldn't! I've got troubles enough. The whole thing's crazy. Doesn't come through regular channels. Just dumped on me. The colonel's no help. Just says if you got here to keep you the hell away from his real soldiers. What in the name of all that ain't holy am I going to do with you?"

Major Pattison was uncomfortably aware of eight men, quiet, somehow remote, watching him. They had an air of being used to this, of being hardened to it, of simply letting it slip past them. They had almost an air of being amused at his version of it, particularly the one in what had the vague appearance of once having been an officer's uniform. He surveyed them again, checking them individually. Scarecrows, yes. An insult to any man's army. But they had a look of lean, stripped-down hardness under those travesties of uniforms and the junk piled on them. Even the short, plump, late-middle-aged one with sleep lines of weariness cutting down under a scraggly, once square-cut beard. His thickening middle was sucked in properly and had a seeming solidness to it. And there was a big one, slab-sided, broad, stolid face apparently a chunk of chipped stone, who looked as if he could heft a black-smith's sledge in either hand and swing them both at once like tack hammers.

Major Pattison leaned forward to massage farther down the leg, head cocked at an angle to look up. "So you're here. Dumped on me. Just dumped. All right, since you're here, you'll work. You think you ever worked before, you'll learn better. There's so all-fired-furious much work piled up here we'll never dig out."

"Christ amighty!" One of them broke out of the quiet, a slender erect one, angry indignation showing on thin, fine-featured face. "Working again! We're supposed to be a fighting unit! Major Foster said—"

"Shut up!" Major Pattison let his own indignation soar into sound. "You'll speak when spoken to! Foster. He's the one started this, ain't he? Dumped you on me. I'd like to have a chance to work him here a while." Major Pattison slapped his game leg. "Fighting! The only fighting I can give you is wrassling with repairs on gov-ernment wagons other damn fools don't have the devil-given sense to use right. Never carry enough grease. Or use it on their hair or something. Never stop at a crossing long enough to soak wheels. Never bother to fix a road. Just slambang along and if anything falls apart let Pattison worry about it. Let Pattison fix it. Pattison is about so all-fired-furious fed up and sick of—"

Major Pattison straightened on his box. "Jesu Becky Maria Sanctissima! I'll have to find you quarters somewhere! And the whole pesty place is jammed already!" He sighed and leaned back against the wall behind him and closed his eyes.

He opened them. A man was speaking, quiet, steady, a trace of a grim, ironic smile on his face. "Don't do any fretting about us, Major." The trace of a smile faded and the man spoke again, stating a fact. "We have tents. Just see we get rations and tell us where to camp. We'll make out."

Major Pattison sighed again. This was a man, according to that confounded letter, who had been busted for outright cowardice. "You're Heath, aren't you? All right, I'll take you at your word. I'll fit you and your men in somewhere soon as a few more buildings are done. Meantime you can pitch camp out beyond the corrals behind here. Out a bit so you won't be in anyone's way. Behave yourselves and I won't be fussing around. Do me a good day's work each day and that's that. For the time being you'll be excused from parade and all that rubbish. The less you're under the colonel's nose the better it'll be for everyone . . ."

It was another of then speaking up now, pushing in, a thickset one with a wide, untrimmed mustache. "Indians! Will we have to watch out for them? All along the trail we've been hearing—"

"Shut up!" Major Pattison exploded. "Yackety bunch, aren't you . . . Indians! Bah! Any Indians you see around here are just sucking around for a little trading and free handouts. You want to tackle any wild ones you have to go looking for them. And run your damn legs off chasing them too. They stay away from here . . ."

Major Pattison started massaging his thigh again. He was aware of eight men watching him, aware too of the somewhat uncomfortable thought that perhaps they were assessing him exactly as he was assessing them. "Jesu Beck!" he said. "Get going. You said you could do it. Do it. Report back here as soon as you get those things you call tents up and something like a camp laid out . . . Jesu Becky Maria! Pattison will see you get rations! Pattison has to do everything around here!"

Major Pattison watched them start away, still in that tight grouping, swinging without a word of command to follow a solid compact man in a dusty patched jacket with the remnants of what might have been stripes on the sleeves. Suddenly he pushed up from his box. "Hold on, Heath!" He started forward, throwing his game leg in it stiff sidewise arc in the gait that could carry him along at a fair clip. "I can still heave my weight around some around this pesty place. Come along. I'll make the quartermaster give you some decent outfits."

Evening. Lights were going out in the completed buildings as Fort Union settled down for the night. Between them and the creek and for a stretch along its banks, in the faint shimmer of a still-new moon, glowed the small, fuel-saving fires of temporary encampments of civilian contractors and their crews, of mule skinners and teamsters resting between long pulls back and forth along the trails, of several emigrant trains halting overnight before starting on westward toward Santa Fe or southwestward toward Rio Abajo, now known as Albuquerque.

Major Pattison stepped quietly out the front door of the upper end unit of the officers' row-houses, which he shared with two captains, bachelors like himself. He eased down from the wide porch or portal that ran along the row, using a cane now in the cloaking dimness of night, angled across the wide roadway that separated the troop area of the fort from the depot and moved along the near side of his quadrangle to the first gateway in. There was no need for this nightly tour of inspection, yet regularly he made it. The quadrangle and what he accomplished there were all that he, with a game leg that troubled him more than he would ever admit, had left out of once stirring ambitions.

Quietly he made his circuit, stopping to stare for a while into the still-glowing embers of the big forge. He moved out of the quadrangle again by the other side and along this to the wide roadway again and turned toward the corrals behind and stopped, oblivious to the restless shiftings of the mules and draft horses there, looking beyond where, small in the distance, dark shadows etched in the dim moonlight, four low tents hunched up from the ground and the last faint glow of a dying fire was pinpointed against the immensity of plain rolling into the far foothills of the Sangre de Cristo mountains.

From his right, from the troop area, came the clear, always melancholy notes of a bugler sounding taps. The notes floated over the fort, drifting away into the vastness of the great vaulted land that stretched away seemingly without limits into nothingness everywhere.

In the hushed silence that followed Major Pattison straightened a bit, listening. For an instant he thought it was an echo. Then, straining toward it, he knew. Someone out there was playing a mouth organ, sounding taps for another fort, infinitely small and isolated, holding its own tiny fragment of shared human strengths and weaknesses against the immensity of an indifferent universe.

"Jesu Becky," said Major Pattison softly, and turned, acutely conscious of his game leg, and started slowly back toward his quarters.

And after the long journeying and whatever may have happened along the route, they were at Fort Union only about two weeks, shade it again a day or two either way.

Here, as before in Virginia, they were unwanted, pushed aside. Unwanted, that is, except by a grumbling brevet major with a stiff leg who was getting work done by them—when they were available.

That was what did it, sent them on, the fact that so often, when the time came for working, one or more of them would not be available. Not the fact itself so much as the reason for it. The unavailable one or ones would be sampling the sparse, hard hospitality of the stone-walled, ten-celled guardhouse that stood conveniently close to the guardroom along the broad avenue fronting the troop barracks. Somehow, by some quirk of circumstance, the past had leaped the months and the miles and was there with them.

Major Pattison knew, of course; had been informed. And the colonel. Neither had any reason to spread the information and, as the event proved, plenty of reason to keep it confidential. But someone spread it, or at least touched off the spreading process. Major Pattison had an orderly who must have had, in ordinary routine of duties, frequent opportunity for unauthorized prying into the major's papers. He remains the best target for any speculation on the point. After all, there is an item in the major's copybook, under date a few months later, that the man had to be transferred on suspicion of pilfering small items from his personal effects.

Within forty-eight hours of their arrival the whole fort knew, perhaps not who they were, but what they were.

"Heath," said Major Pattison. "I can't exactly blame a man for fighting when someone calls him a coward. But those men of yours must go around asking for it. Too all-fired-furious-touchy altogether. Five times I've had to go talk myself billy-blue in the face to pull some of them out of hock. Five times up to yesterday. Now it's another one. Young Fulton. Right when I need that harness job he's been doing. I thought he was safe anyway. So blinking-damned-mousy-quiet. Sent him over to the depot a while ago for something. He didn't come back. Now I hear he's cooling off in the cell I got Kinsey out of yesterday. Climbed right over a counter after somebody who probably just flipped an eye at him . . ."

Major Pattison looked up from his shaded box at the man standing in front of him, a right solid soldierly shape of a man in a decent, still-new work outfit with the regulation stripes of a sergeant on the sleeves of his blouse and a right-steady, competent hand at the forge feeding hot iron under the hammer of a big, slab-sided private who plainly was quite ready at any moment to keep on quietly working or to spit in the eye of the whole damned world at a word from him. An aggravating, baffling man too, beyond reach, wrapped in a relentless self-reliance, plainly a thorough soldier with training and experience behind him, yet strangely and subtly unmilitary, giving the feeling that he confronted a major exactly as he would confront a private or a general or any individual in the entire roster of the race, that rank and authority and the respect due them were simply things to be endured, observed, and meaningless in any final balancing of accounts.

Major Pattison began to massage his thigh. Why did he have this urge to get at the man, to break through to him, not as an officer bending down from superior position, but as another human being worrying to the best of limited ability through the shortening span of life. Not just because the man knew so surprisingly much about metalwork and had stepped up production at the forge with the same callous, indifferent efficiency with which he did everything assigned him. There was a tightness, a tension, hidden in him, hidden behind that iron self-control, a suggestion that single and alone in his own deliberate isolation he grappled with the far secret core of existence.

Major Pattison sighed. "Yes, I know, Heath. It's another case of let Pattison fix it. Pattison can do it. Pattison can hand out a good line of guff. Pattison can talk his throat raw and promise to lay on extra work till young Fulton hasn't the energy left to make trouble. But Jesu Becky, Heath, I'm telling you Pattison is up to the gullet full of this business. You know what they're calling you now? Pattison's pets! And the colonel—"

Major Pattison stopped, aware that he was talking to himself. The man was standing there, properly respectful, properly listening, but the words meant nothing to him. They hit against some hardness in him and they meant nothing.

"Jesu Becky Maria, man!" said Major Pattison. "Do you think I don't know you could control your men if you wanted to? You'd never have got them all the way out here if you couldn't! Yes, they take a ragging. But they could stand it if you'd make them. They ought to be used to it by now anyway. And it'd die out soon enough if they'd hang on and take it. I don't blame them. I blame you. You're their officer. You're not playing square with me. And you're failing them."

"No!" The man was speaking and Major Pattison saw the cold flame lighting his eyes. "No! They've taken it long enough! They didn't come two thousand miles out here to repair wagons!"

Major Pattison leaned forward to massage farther down his leg, staring at the ground before him. He had the strange feeling that suddenly roles had been reversed, that he no longer sat in judgment, that this man was judging him and perhaps finding failure. "Repairing wagons is all I'm good for now," he said softly, conscious that he spoke as no officer ever needed to speak to a man in the ranks, and troubled, but not by that fact.

Major Pattison sighed again and pushed up from his box. "Get on back to the forge, Heath. And don't worry about Fulton. Pattison will do it."

Midmorning of another day. Major Pattison limped into the quadrangle, face pale and determined. He limped over by the forge where Sergeant Jared Heath fed hot iron under the awkward hammer of a heavyset civilian worker who claimed to be a blacksmith.

"Heath! Round up your men and bring them to me on the double!"

Major Pattison limped to his box and sat down upon it and began to massage his leg, waiting . . .

He looked up at the tight grouping before him. He was definitely an officer, disgusted, determined. "Seven of you. Quite right. I know only too well that Mr. Zattig is now occupying the cell previously honored by Misters Fulton and Geary and Kinsey. Twice, as I recall, by Mr. Kinsey. Next to that once honored by Mr. Merriam. I am surprised that Misters Webb and Selous have not yet tried them. Just waiting their turns, I suppose . . . Well, the colonel has not taken kindly to the fact that three of his men had to be led to the hospital for repairs this morning. He has informed me that he will no longer extend the hospitality of his guardhouse or any other portion of the entire reservation to any of you. A source of infection he called you. Very apt. On his authority I am going to quarantine you where, I hope, you can do the least possible damage. A supply train is making up for Fort Bascom, leaving within the hour. You are going with it. Captain Clark there is always yipping for men. He can have you."

Major Pattison surveyed the seven of his eight special-duty responsibilities. They stood as before, quiet, remote, watching him, taking their cue from that damned aggravating man with those unimportant, unnecessary stripes on his sleeves, and he felt an urge to grasp them as a group and shake them into the realization that he too lived and breathed and had to face up to the limitations of his own existence. If only they had not come carrying that sorry past with them, they might have eased the pressure in his quadrangle for him. And which one of them was it played that dim-damned harmonica? He did not even know that. A sense of failure was strong in him.

"Jesu Becky Maria Sanctissima!" said Major Pattison. "That's the best I can do for you! The colonel was all for splitting you apart and tossing you all over the territory! That'd take time, finagling with Washington! So I'm pushing you out from under his nose!"

That damned aggravating man was looking at him now, seeing him, recognition of him as another living breathing individual far back in the clean, cold eyes. Major Pattison straightened on his box. "All right. Get moving. Strike that camp of yours. I'll send for Zattig."

Major Pattison watched them go, swinging to follow their man, and a sudden pain stabbed into his consciousness. Abruptly he realized that he was gripping his game leg, hard, deliberately hurting himself. Gently he began to massage the leg and the thought crept into his mind that he had been used, that a compact, square-shouldered man, unknown to him two weeks before, had judged him, assessed him, and used him, and with the thought, paradoxically, he felt better. He pushed up from his box to send a message to the guardhouse and to limp to his quarters and write a note to Captain Clark.

It took four, sometimes five days in good weather, a widely varying number in bad, for light wagons—heavy and heavily loaded vans could not yet make the rough stretch past Hatch's Ranch—to cover the one hundred forty-five miles southeastward from Fort Union to Fort Bascom in that year 1864. And that was a reasonably good trail as trails ran then in that vast unsettled, and in part even unexplored, region where the vegas of New Mexico merged into the Llano Estacado of what had finally been established as the Texas Panhandle.

The trail was lowland most of the way, well-watered—a vital consideration in the Southwest—because it followed waterways: eastward down the valley of the Mora to its junction with the Canadian; southward along the Canadian to where Conchas Dam now impounds the waters for irrigation; then eastward again along the turning, widening, treacherous, quicksanded Canadian in the footsteps of Coronado and other early Spanish conquistadors who, long before the first colonies troubled the east coast of the continent, had passed and repassed this way in search of Quivira and its fabled cities of gold.

There, cradled in a curve of the constantly twisting Canadian, close to where Pajarito Creek comes in from the south, about ten miles due north of the historic, high, dark butte, the famous Apache lookout and landmark known out of dim, traceless antiquity to the tribes of the region as Tucumcari, a tight-lipped, frustrated army captain had been trying for almost exactly a year to establish a fort.

He had a name for it, officially designated in honor of Captain George N. Bascom, killed in action at Valverde on the Rio Grande below Socorro during Sibley's invasion in early 1862. He had orders for its construction, officially issued in August, 1863, in response to pleas for another outpost against Comanche raiding, complete with plans for sturdy brick-and-stone buildings, neatly grouped, to accommodate a post depot and two full companies, one of infantry, and one of cavalry, with all the usual appurtenances of shops and storehouses and hospital and guardhouse and officers' quarters and laundresses' quarters and sheltered corrals and surrounding bastioned wall. After a year of zeal and good intentions, what he actually had in existence was a collection of temporary jacal or upright-logged buildings with leaky, timber-and-branch-and-dirt roofs, a few temporary poled corrals, and a fair start on two storehouses, these at least being built according to the plan and, though still unfinished, already in use, one for shops and offices, the other for stores and guardroom.

His trouble was that his superiors, perhaps at Fort Union, certainly at General Carleton's headquarters in Santa Fe and even more certainly in far-off Washington, had the quaint, obtuse notion that most of the work could and should be done by the enlisted men under his command. That was virtually impossible except at a slow, sporadic pace, for the obvious reason that these same enlisted men were also expected to protect the area against Indian depredations. Much of the time most of his garrison would be, in the worn official phrase, "absent on detached service," running down reports and rumors of scattered attacks, escorting wagon trains through possibly dangerous regions, chasing Indians who led them with monotonous regularity into rugged, waterless wastelands, occasionally indulged in a few brief skirmishes, then simply faded into the vastness of the landscape.

He might not have been so zealous, this Captain Clark, had he known that just six years later Fort Bascom, at last in the postwar years with their release of manpower beginning to approximate the original ambitious plans, would be abandoned by a prodigal government, left to be stripped of everything movable by settlers arriving to found in time the present town of Tucumcari and to weather away in the endless winds of the Southwest until only a few low mounds would mark the lines of once sturdy walls. He did not know this. He had a command of his own insulated against any frequent ranking interference by many miles of rolling plain and intervening ridge and mesa, and he was determined to make a good showing. And along in the latter days of August a train of light wagons arrived at his fort bringing some of the grain he had requested to supplement grazing forage for his hard-worked mules, some of the replacement tools he had been expecting for six months or more, and some of the hardware he needed. And bringing him eight extra, unexpected, footsore men. And a note from Major Pattison . . .

Here is a loss that hurts. What did Major Pattison say in that note? On the evidence of what happened, developed, it tipped the scale of circumstance, first in favor of a practical working arrangement between the captain and his new men and second, and more important, rising from that first, in favor of a chance for a man named Jared Heath to lead his queer, crippled, rag-tail company straight and unswerving into the ultimate testing he sought. But what the major wrote beyond the bare, certain information he must have included is gone beyond recovery.

This, however, is known: Captain Clark read that note and grunted something unintelligible and put his eight new men to work at once building themselves a jacal shelter and when he had the unloading of the wagons well under way he retired to the corner of one of the unfinished storehouses he was using as an office and read that note again and sat on a camp stool studying what it said and sent for the one of the eight with the stripes of a sergeant on his sleeves.

"At ease, Sergeant," said Captain Clark in a tone that plainly implied not-too-damned-much-at-ease. "I have here a most interesting document. Anybody else wrote it I'd think he was off his rocker. But I know Pattison. So I intend to make myself perfectly clear. This is not Fort Union. This is a godforsaken post out at the end of nowhere and there is no place here for men who can't fit in and pull their weight with the rest."

Captain Clark studied the man facing him, probably beginning to be aware that he was making no impression whatsoever.

"Get this straight, Sergeant. I am not interested in the past. What happened back East happened back East. You and your men will have your own quarters. You may have your own mess. Otherwise I propose to treat you exactly as I do everyone else. I will expect you and your—well, your company—to be on the color line for roll call each morning and to carry your share of guard duty and policing of this post in proper rotation. I will expect you to do each day what you are told to do, promptly and with no malingering."

Captain Clark paused. He looked down at the note in his hands and waggled it thoughtfully between his fingers and looked up again at the man facing him, probably aware that he had not as yet come even close to the real problem, perhaps considering, under the impact of the man, an alteration in tactics.

"Sergeant. I will make a bargain with you. You keep your men in line and give me honest work on this fort and I will see that, when or if the opportunity comes, you and your men do a bit more than—well, what you might call repairing wagons . . . Do I make myself clear?"

"Very clear, sir," said Sergeant Jared Heath.

And during the next weeks, as August slipped into September and September into October and the high plains country held unchanged the sun-drenched, windswept wonder of its days, yielding to the changing season only in the sharp chill of its nights, there was no outbreak of fighting at Fort Bascom, no need for the guardhouse that was not yet built. There was, instead, work and work and more work. Patrols came and went and a detachment chased down a rumor that two boys had been scalped alive over near the Texas line and dragged back with the report that the scalping was intentional but the leaving of them alive was not and the perpetrators were uncaught and unidentified Comanche braves and another detachment went scurrying upcountry after more Comanches who had attacked a wagon train and killed five men near Lower Cimarron Springs and dragged back with the usual report of a trail followed and lost.

And Company Q, with the aid of a squat, stout wagon and a four-mule pull, made bricks and bricks and more bricks.

Old inspection sheets refer to the buildings at Fort Bascom as adobe-walled. The adobes used were not the usual variety, large and flat, weighing some thirty to forty pounds each, made of what appears to the outlander to be ordinary mud, sunbaked. Those made and used at Fort Bascom were smaller, more like regular somewhat oversize eastern bricks. They were made of sandstone hauled from the base of the sharp bluff just across the river where flood waters, swinging around the big curve that cradled the fort, had washed and worn and carved for centuries. It was a semisoft crumbling sandstone and it was crushed, worked with water and straw to the proper consistency, slapped into forms and crude-kiln-baked into bricks.

Very little can be traced about those weeks. But the brickmaking stands out.

We made bricks. Ten thousand million goddamned bricks. And made them right.

And one other activity remains, observed by Captain Clark and told later to Major Pattison, who recorded it briefly in his copybook.

A Sunday, probably the first after their arrival, in the afternoon, the only sizable stretch of free time in the whole week for most of the men. Captain Clark sat in the unroofed but stout-walled new building that would be a barrack, estimating the fittings he would need to finish it. Through an opening that would be a window he could see some of his men watching and becoming boisterous over a horseshoe match between picked champions of the infantry and the cavalry. Quietly he went on with his listing, padding it in the cynical certainty that he would never get all he requested.

He looked up from the paper on his knees. The men outside by the temporary corrals were moving away, not drifting idly as at the end of a match, but purposefully, some leading and others straggling and all in the same direction. He rose and stepped to the opening that would be the main doorway. They were moving toward the river, angling toward the screen of low trees and bushes that masked a level stretch of bank. They stopped, close by the bushes, surprisingly silent, and seemed to be peering at something beyond.

Striding swiftly, Captain Clark covered the distance between. He too stopped and peered through the bushes. There, on the level stretch beyond, he saw it, Company Q, all eight of them, in full outfits, knapsacks on backs, canteens and cartridge boxes and bayonets at waists, rifles on shoulders, drilling. Faintly a rough, heartwarming voice, rumbling in a big throat, came to him.

"Are ye all dead? Get some snap in them knees, ye lameback mules! To the rear . . . march!"

Smartly, like one man, Company Q halted in stride, spun on its toes, and swung into stride again, heading back across the level stretch. And again the voice: "Fulton, me boy, give us the tune."

Without breaking rhythm, moving steadily with the others, the third man in the front row handed his rifle to the fourth and fumbled in a jacket pocket and raised both hands to his mouth. Captain Clark stared in amazement. Not since his time in military institute in Pennsylvania, years and years ago, had he heard that tune. Jaunty, defiant, it drifted to him. "The Rogue's March." He heard himself humming the words under his breath.

Poor—old—sol—dier.
Poor—old—sol—dier.
He'll be tarred and feathered and sent to hell
Because he wouldn't soldier well . . .

Captain Clark caught hold of himself with a start. He remembered his own men lined out behind the bushes beside him, remembered remarks from them overheard the last few days and the tight, stiff faces of Company Q hearing them too. Then he noticed that his men were staying quietly behind the bushes, watching, listening, and staying there. And then he heard one of them, unconscious of his presence, mutter to another in a low, rough tone with an edging of affectionate respect.

"Look at them busted bastards. Look at 'em step."

With a soft grunt of relief Captain Clark returned to the bare-walled, roofless barrack and his cynical, hopeful listing.

And meanwhile, during those weeks, circumstances were shaping toward a chance for Captain Clark too to redeem his bargain . . .

The plains tribes were increasingly active that year, particularly in the summer and early fall, particularly along the Santa Fe Trail through Kansas and Colorado and down into New Mexico. That can be labeled as most people labeled it then, as an example of their unrestrained, uncivilized savagery. They were taking advantage, so states the usual explanation, of the fact that the white men were fighting each other in a great Civil War with garrison after garrison of the frontier forts drained for the fighting in the East. And no doubt they were. But there were other factors involved too. The Civil War had not halted or slowed, at times seemed even to have increased, the number of emigrant trains heading directly through the Indian country and the number of settlers encroaching on Indian land. The dwindling of the buffalo herds was already becoming apparent. Moreover, the Indians were not receiving treaty-promised annuities for the loss of lands and the dwindling of the buffalo herds with anything approaching regularity and in the amounts and quality stipulated. And another repetition of an old familiar story had just occurred in 1863, poisoning relations down through the Southwest in 1864.

Two Comanche and one plains Apache and four Kiowa chiefs had gone to Washington and there signed a treaty renewing that of ten years before in which they agreed to permit safe travel on the Santa Fe Trail in exchange for $25,000 in annuity goods. They returned, taking word to their tribes. And back in Washington Congress refused to bother itself with ratifying the treaty and appropriating the money—and Indians going to the agencies for the goods received nothing but explanations that meant to them only further proof that the white men talked with double tongues and made promises with no intention of fulfilling them.

What seems to have set off the campaigns of late 1864 was an incident at Fort Larned in Kansas. A number of Kiowas were camped near the fort holding a scalp dance to celebrate a raid led by White Bear down into Texas. They had little reason to know that the whites in the fort would be upset by such activity. Those same whites were engaged in a war with the Texans, weren't they? But those whites seem to have been definitely upset and nervous at news of the dance. Two Kiowas went to the fort entrance, probably intending to go to the sutler's store as they had often done before. The sentry ordered them away. They did not speak English, were used to making out with sign talk. They kept right on. The sentry raised his gun. They understood that language readily enough. One of them, with the speed and precision for which his tribe was well known, promptly drove two arrows into him and the two Kiowas dashed away. There was immediate excitement in the fort, the entire garrison being turned out to repel a supposed attack, while the Kiowas, noting this activity, prudently struck their camp and faded away. As they faded, they took with them most of the cavalry horses, which were grazing outside the fort. And then White Bear, known to the whites as Satanta, added the final touch. He sent a message to the fort commander to provide better horses thereafter. Those just received were not much good. And he and his Kiowas headed southward to the Llano Estacado and joined a large camp of Comanches at Red Bluff on the Canadian River. While they waited there for any further developments, a Comanche named Little Buffalo improved the time by gathering a big war party from both groups and leading a highly successful raid deeper into Texas.

The Union war department, though probably not too much incensed at such raiding in Texas, was apparently convinced that a general Indian "war" had started. What troops were available in the territories were ordered into action, three campaigns at once, one in Kansas, one in Colorado, and one into Texas out of New Mexico. That in Kansas was sidetracked, given new orders to get after Quantrell's raiders. That in Colorado led to a black day in late November when a Colonel J. M. Chivington blasted his own career and converted the Cheyennes into the deadliest, for their number, foes the whites would have on the plains in the brutal, infamous massacre of an unsuspecting, "friendly" Cheyenne village at Sand Creek. That into Texas out of New Mexico led head-on into one of the biggest Indian battles ever fought.

General Carleton, still ruling the territory under martial law, was at the time still busy with his own campaigns against the Apaches and the Navajos. Right at the beginning he had decided that territorial Colonel Christopher Carson of the First New Mexico Volunteers, living quietly up at Taos after brief participation in the troubles of Sibley's invasion, was the man for active field command. Colonel Carson, who had long since forgotten more about Indians than Carleton would ever learn and still knew more than any other man in the territory, being an honest man and always honest in his dealings with them whether in trade or treaty or down the sights of a gun, was reluctant to take the assignment. He believed that more understanding and some honest treaty-making would do the job without the use of gunpowder. At last, under pressure, he accepted. Once having accepted, handicapped by Carleton's policies, bound by Carleton's orders, he had been forced to make efficient use of considerable gunpowder.

The Apaches, except for small groups in far mountain fastnesses, had been rounded up and brought to temporary terms. The same was being done with the Navajos, a much more numerous tribe, and General Carleton was having them herded into a concentration camp at Bosque Redondo with, as could have been expected, starvation and disease rampant there. Now he had in hand orders to do something more than mere patrol work about the Comanches and Kiowas, who were reported to be encamped somewhere over in the Texas Panhandle, probably along the

Canadian. He and his staff made their plans. They sent orders to Colonel Carson to take time from the Navajo roundup and take command of a punitive expedition. They scratched about and found they could spare some units from the territorial and the California regiments still in New Mexico. They checked over their military maps and ordered those units to rendezvous on or about November 4 at Fort Bascom.

From Fort Union up in the valley of the Mora, from Fort Sumner over on the upper Pecos, they came, troopers swinging in their saddles in long columns along the trails, infantrymen plodding through the distances of the wide vegas, supply wagons grumbling, groaning over the rough passages of the intervening hills. And down from the highlands above Taos, bringing their weapons and their war paint, came Indian scouts, mountain Indians, Utes and Jicarilla Apaches. They knew the commander of this campaign. He had been their agent for a time back along the years. They knew him. They would fight with him against the plains raiders on the promise of plunder.

By the time the commander arrived, the first week in November, his forces had assembled, thirteen other officers including an assistant surgeon, two hundred twenty cavalrymen, seventy-five infantrymen, and twenty-five artillerymen with two twelve-pounder mountain howitzers. He would need that little battery. And seventy-two Utes and Apaches, tagged by two wrinkled, ancient squaws.

That was not all he had expected, hoped for, planned for. General Carleton's original scheme had included the recruiting of a considerable number of Navajos from the concentration camp at Bosque Redondo. Many were willing, ready to do anything to escape from the crowded suffering there. But the Utes would not fight in company with their own traditional enemies, the Navajos. And the Utes, at this particular time, were more to be trusted than the Navajos.

The various camps spread out around Fort Bascom, along the river. The fort itself, what there was of it, was the center of bustling seemingly confused activity. And there, where one day would be a much better equipped blacksmith shop, eight men worked at and around a forge rigged with callous, indifferent efficiency out of scant materials by a man named Jared Heath, repairing wagons.

Captain Clark stopped nearby. With him was a smallish, wiry man whose sandy hair above cold, blue eyes and drooping, sandy mustache was graying rapidly now. He wore what had been and was still vaguely recognizable as a colonel's uniform with the air of a man who had little use for uniforms and all they might represent. Captain Clark said something to him and he looked at the eight men working, repairing wagons, his quiet, patient glance moving over them. One of them raised his head and the eyes met his, eyes unlike his own, eyes dark and deep under the dark hair, and yet like his, like those of the best of the mountain men, the early original mountain men he had known as old men in his youth in the fur-trapping days in the lonely mountains above the little town known then as Don Fernando de Taos, the look in them straight, strong, and clear and clean and cold.

"Cap'n," said Colonel Kit Carson, turning to move on. "They look like men to me."

And on the morning of the sixth the command moved out, fording the river to the north side in it a jumble of splashing difficulties, and stretched out into shape eastward toward Texas, the Indian scouts jogging ahead, the cavalry next in long, jingling column, and the little battery with its mule-team howitzers and its men trudging beside, and the twenty-seven four-mule wagons of the supply train and the one ambulance allotted the expedition, and the infantry plodding steadily behind. And there, with the supply train, on the driver's seats of the first four wagons, two to a seat, were the eight men of Company Q, teamsters again, serving without any official recognition in recorded orders under a smallish, wiry man who was heading into dangerous country, deliberately looking for a fight.

Six

They camped that night where Ute Creek joins the Canadian and shook down into the routine of camp duties that would hold the rest of the way. Many days and many miles of marching were ahead but already the tingle of campaign tension was taking hold of the men, a strangeness hovering over them. For most of them this was new country, a new kind of country, an advance against a new kind of enemy. They had served before, and against Indians, but chiefly in the Rio Grande Valley, against the lowland Apaches and the Navajos, who fought mostly on foot and in scattered groups. Now they were moving out into limitless, seemingly landmarkless vegas, moving against the short, stocky, broad-faced, superb-on-horseback Comanches, the lords of the south plains who were wringing from grudging officers the admission they were among the finest light cavalry the world had ever known, and their daring, deadly, arrogant cousins, the Kiowas.

The Indians with the command added to the strangeness. Already, that first night, they were beginning their traditional war party program that would keep them at high pitch for all dangers encountered and any opportunity to grasp honor in battle. Grouped around their own campfire, they counted coups far into the night, voices rising to the throbbing of drums, and at times leaped to their feet to chant and stamp dances of war, and the strange and, to white ears, alien sounds drifted on the night winds over the entire encampment. They were on the warpath with Father Kit, the only agent who had ever understood them, the man who had never lied to them, who had fought them and lived with them and knew them and who could, were he so minded, count more coups than any one of them, and they would lead him to the fighting he wanted.

For Father Kit himself this was not new country. And what country anywhere in the Southwest and on far northward, now in his last years, would be new to him, the last true representative of the mountain men who had opened the larger half of a continent. Years ago he had worked for William Bent, traveling often down through this region from Bent's Old Fort on the Arkansas. Once, down this way with a few companions, he had lost all his animals to raiders and had to tramp the long trail back through hostile territory on foot. And again, after a Comanche war party attack on a wagon train near where Fort Union now stood, he had pulled together an avenging posse and trailed the warriors for days along this very route and attacked and destroyed their camp . . .

In the morning the command stretched out again, establishing the daytime routine that would be followed long day after long day. Two Indian scouts rode on ahead several hours before the column itself pushed into motion. They would not be seen again until evening, when they would return, disdaining to speak to anyone else, reporting directly to Father Kit. And when the column itself began to move, more Indian scouts would ride out far-ranging on the flanks. There was some grumbling in the ranks, among some of the officers too, at this dependence on cussed Injuns against ambush or surprise attack. But Father Kit, in his patient way, paid no attention to it. He knew his Utes, his Apaches.

He knew too where he was going. On ahead, almost across the Texas Panhandle, close to the borders of the Indian Nations, were the ruins of a private fort and trading post, established many years ago by William Bent, known as Adobe Walls. Somewhere beyond, the Comanches and Kiowas would be in winter camps. He would make the old abandoned post his headquarters. The still standing walls would shelter his wagons and rations and ammunition and he would carry the supplies needed for swift slashing forays from there on the packsaddles lashed now on top of some of the wagons . . .

Ten days they marched eastward along an ancient, long, unused Mexican "road" paralleling the Canadian. Josiah Gregg had passed this way, in the opposite direction, on his first trip to Santa Fe and had written of it in his *Commerce of the Prairies*. On the tenth day they reached the Cañada de los Ruedes, the Canyon of the Wheels, where old-time Mexican trains, heading for trade in the States, had halted to repair broken wheels with wood from the relatively large trees there. The old "road" turned to the north here and they left it and pushed on eastward, finding and following an ancient Indian trail which again paralleled the Canadian.

Nine more days, held always to the pace of the tramping infantrymen and the artillerymen whose gun carriages were too small for any riding, and they reached Mule Spring and went into camp early in the afternoon. Adobe Walls was not far ahead, perhaps no more than a short day's march, but too far to be reached before well into dark. Tempers were short and there was much bickering among the men. The long rising tension had been tightened toward the intolerable by the long, monotonous advance into the unknown unrelieved by any sight or sound of the menace sought that must be lurking somewhere in the silent, ever-surrounding vastness, grown monstrous in imagination fed on the tales around the campfires at night. And just as the sun was setting all that was swept away in a few brief moments and they were soldiers again, steady under orders, caught in the alerting excitement of actuality overtaken at last.

The Utes, the Apaches, knew it first. They were lounging around the camp, waiting to join in the soldiers' mess, some of them apparently dozing, yet suddenly they leaped to their feet, staring intently eastward, talking excitedly in their own languages. They had seen, or sensed, what none of the white men could see yet even when pointed out to them, the two forward scouts, still miles away, racing their ponies toward the camp. And they had read, in the manner of the riding, the message.

Officers and men crowded around the commander, shouting questions.

"I reckon," said Colonel Kit Carson, "they found us some Comanche over thar."

What they had found, about ten miles ahead, between the command and Adobe Walls, was a broad, beaten trail made that very morning by many Indians moving with large herds of horses and cattle. The scouts had read the sign as a white man might a newspaper. Kiowas mostly, with some Comanches, and these had not moved hurriedly, in alarm. Probably they had simply been changing their camp, their temporary village, to a fresh site because the grass around it had been grazed thin. They would not have traveled far, not in the one day, not with those herds. And what that meant was that Colonel Carson had to change his plan. Within a matter of minutes he had the situation in hand. No establishing of headquarters now at Adobe Walls before mounting an attack.

These Indians might still be between the command and the old post. There was every chance they were still unaware any soldiers were near. So be it. The cavalry and the howitzer battery would move out with him in light marching order immediately after a quick meal and follow the trail found and if possible attack in the early dawn before their presence was known. The infantry under Captain Ahearn would remain to guard the supply train, which would wait until morning, then follow and keep coming until it overtook the rest of the command.

As dusk settled over the camp and the last light of the sun below the horizon flung the unbelievable beauty of a plains sunset across the vast empty land through which they had come, Colonel Carson led his mounted men, Indians and cavalry, and his priceless, indispensable, little battery, three hundred thirty men in all, eastward toward battle. And there, left behind, were one commissioned officer and seventy-five infantrymen and the regular teamsters. And Company Q, left behind too, out of it again . . .

Out of the biggest Indian battle to be fought in the Southwest. Not a battle that would achieve the fame of others like Custer's misnamed Last Stand, which was not a stand but a forewarned, foolish, fumbling, deliberate attack that deserved to meet disaster. There were no newspaper or magazine correspondents in the territory to write glowing accounts of this one. It was fought at a time when the final rising crescendo of the Civil War in the East monopolized public attention. There was no halo of annihilation to give it special prominence. It was led by a man who could neither read nor write and had no pipelines to publicity and, even having them, would have snorted at the thought of using them. He was ordered to lead a punitive expedition and he took what units were available and pushed out into enemy country some two hundred miles from the nearest possible relief post and with a much smaller force bumped straight into as many and probably considerably more and as able warriors as Custer did on the Bighorn, was licked to a standstill and sent into retreat and personally always admitted as much despite the mild glow of victory whoever wrote (and obviously pruned and edited) his report for him put upon it—and yet pulled the majority of his men safely through. And despite the licking, the unmistakable standoff, the imperative long retreat back to Fort Bascom, he achieved his purpose. He had given the southern plains raiders a strong taste of what a small force, determined, held-together, well-led, could do even against ten times overwhelming numbers. That small force had killed and wounded more warriors—not women and children too, as Chivington was doing at Sand Creek, as Custer would do later at the Washita, but warriors—than were killed and wounded in any other Indian battle. The chiefs must have talked that over in their councils and decided, temporarily at least, that there was wisdom in not inviting the possible dispatch against them of a larger force. Along in January of the new year, less than two months after the battle, two months during which the emigrant and supply trails were quiet, a Comanche chief, suitably escorted, appeared at Fort Bascom under a flag of truce and started negotiations for a new treaty.

Out of that battle, yes. Together with one commissioned officer and seventy-five infantrymen and some teamsters. But not out of their own brief, bloody skirmish.

The striking force moved out, quiet, cautious, under strict orders forbidding any talking or smoking, the Indian scouts wrapped in their buffalo robes, the troopers in their overcoats, against the chill cold of night that was whitening the grasses with frost. Near midnight they swung over to drop into the immediate valley of the Canadian and came upon the deep, still-fresh trail of the enemy, plain even in the darkness. There they dismounted, holding their horses by the bridles, and waited, chilled through, silent, waiting for the first thin streakings of dawn.

Time passed, slow, cold, inexorable, and the dim promise of light, wan and gray, edged up the sky from the far horizon ahead and they mounted and moved forward and the fact of movement had barely begun to warm chilled muscles when they heard shouts on the opposite side of the river, startled, challenging, and they knew they were discovered, had reached the enemy's outlying pickets. Instantly the Indians with the command whirled their horses into a large clump of chaparral and shed their robes, hiding them there, and emerged stripped and painted for war, and dashed in seeming wild disorder into the river toward the opposite bank and Colonel Carson, issuing orders in his patient, unhurried way, sent most of his cavalry splashing across after them. A few shots and the pickets, three of them, were racing down the valley with the scouts and cavalry in pursuit. In a few moments, despite the growing light of dawn, they were all lost to sight, hidden by distance and the clumps of low trees and the tall grasses of the valley, shoulder high in places to a man on a horse, and Colonel Carson, calculating in his knowledge of the country the probable location of the village, headed on down the valley on the near side of the river and the remainder of his cavalry and the slow-moving, little battery with him.

That must have been hard, chest-aching work for the men of the battery, on foot, hurrying as best they could under constant urging from their officer, youngish Lieutenant Pettis, who years later, living then in far-off Rhode Island, would write an account of this battle.

The quick, sharp command, "TROT—MARCH," would be given to the battery, which would move out at a trot for a few

hundred yards, when the dismounted cannoneers would soon be
left stringing out a long way to the rear; "WALK—MARCH,"
would be resumed, so as to allow the men to regain their places,
and after allowing then a short time to regain their breath, the
same movements would be again and again performed.

Hours of this—or so it seemed. Actually not quite two. Firing could be heard ahead, on their side of the river again, constantly receding. Batches of the Kiowas' cattle were passed and some of the Indians of the command were seen, each herding a number of captured horses off in a separate group which he would leave to be reclaimed later as personal plunder after selecting a fresh horse now to replace his original tired mount for a return to the fight.

The sun was up, throwing its light in glorious streamers along the valley, melting the frost on the grasses, and on forward where a low hill butted out almost to the river was the Kiowa village, the whitened lodges fooling Lieutenant Pettis for a moment into the belief they were army tents. It was apparently deserted and still the firing was well ahead, on beyond, still receding. The scouts and the cavalry had swept up to the village on the heels of the pickets and the Kiowa warriors, grabbing their weapons and the few favorite horses tethered in the village overnight, had made a brief, desperate defense while the women and children scurried into the hills off to the left and had retreated then on down the valley fighting a stubborn, delaying action. And old Tohauson, great chief of all the Kiowas, known to the whites as Little Mountain, had swung his still-sturdy, aging bones astride a stout pony and gone in headlong gallop on downstream, past the old ruins of Adobe Walls, to warn other and larger villages there.

That was the unforeseen, the unanticipated, which made this battle not simply the first of a series against groups of the enemy as found but the only battle of the campaign, not a relatively short encounter with a single camp or temporary village but a daylong increasing struggle that would send the command into retreat. What it had stumbled upon was a spreading network of winter villages, a concentration within riding distance of thousands of Kiowas and Comanches and plains Apaches and even some visiting Cheyennes and Arapahoes. Ah, that priceless indispensable little battery of twelve-pound howitzers.

That battery was coming on, fast as the panting cannoneers could drag tiring legs, on to the apparently deserted village—not really deserted, because the two ancient squaws who had come with the scouts were hunting through the lodges and finding four old people, blind and crippled, unable to get away, and were dispatching them with hand axes, an action which would bring down upon them, when he heard of it, the wrath of Father Kit. And the battery plugged on, straight through the village, on down the valley after the cavalry, and far ahead at last they could see what was happening.

The advance force had reached Adobe Walls. The cavalry had sheltered their horses within the ruins and were out beyond deployed on the ground as skirmishers. In front of them an Indian battle was in full swing, not particularly effective in deadliness in the white man's manner of war, but magnificent in horsemanship and daring. The scouts, mounted and riding as only Indians could ride, with the reckless, amazing assurance of absolute mastery, were dashing forward and back and forward again against about an equal number of Kiowas and Comanches who were doing the same, swooping down along the sides of their mounts in full gallop and firing under the horses' necks. And beyond this individualized duel, probably holding back from it to keep the immediate odds about even in deference to the daring of the scouts, but obviously massing for an attack on the command as a whole, were many more than a thousand warriors with their chiefs riding up and down, stirring them to battle pitch.

Colonel Carson galloped forward, leaving the battery behind, the detachment of cavalry that had been escorting it with him. He rode to the top of a small rise close to the ruins. Not a mile away he could see another enemy village, five hundred and more lodges, and more warriors coming from it and yet others in the far distance approaching. Patient, unhurried, he studied the scene. He looked back. Lieutenant Pettis and his battery were straining near. He smiled grimly at the earnest, youngish man and issued the one order that has been preserved verbatim out of the whole day's doings: "Pettis, throw a few shell into that crowd over thar."

Yes, that priceless, indispensable, little battery. Without it the entire command might in time have been overwhelmed, wiped out. Even if they had managed to hold out behind the protection of Adobe Walls, they might never have broken out and accomplished the retreat to Fort Bascom. It was that battery, shells short-ranged but with wide explosive power, that kept the enemy, as a body, at a distance. No doubt many, perhaps most, of these Indians had seen or at least knew about the white man's artillery. But they were astonished at the sudden appearance of those two twelve-pounders way out there in their own territory. They soon learned to watch for the shells and avoid them. But they soon learned too that it was hazardous to gather in large groups within range. It was that battery which held them to scattered action, to sniping and skirmishing and constant harassing by warriors acting singly or in small groups . . . At the first shot all those within sight straightened on their horses, staring in amazement. By the fourth shot not a one was within range.

And still the command was not fully aware of what it had

stumbled into. In the brief interval of relative quiet with the enemy withdrawal after those first shells, Colonel Carson ordered a halt to enable his men to water their horses at the little creek behind Adobe Walls (later to be known as Carson Creek) and to breakfast on the scant rations in their haversacks. After breakfast they would push on under cover of the howitzers and take the second village there ahead of them.

That was the plan. He never even tried to put it into operation. Before the men had finished chewing their raw bacon and hardtack the enemy had taken the initiative and they were pinned down, compelled to deploy again in battle line out around the ruins. Kiowas and Comanches and plains Apaches by the hundreds, dismounted, were hiding in the tall grasses, creeping close, and maintaining a hot fire. Hundreds more, fresh-mounted, were charging back and forth past the line, firing under their animals' necks. The daring of these dashes astounded even Colonel Carson. He had never seen the cussed devils fight quite like this. Old Tohauson himself, Little Mountain, charged in along the very muzzles of the troopers' guns and had his horse shot under him and ran back and mounted another and came again. Stumbling Bear, one of the younger chiefs, wore his little daughter's shawl for good luck and had it. He counted thirteen bullet holes in that shawl that night. And all the while more Indians were arriving from the villages on down the river. Not all had guns but these were Indians who could often drop a buffalo with a single arrow and could have three or four in the air while a trooper was loading and firing once.

The whole region swarmed with them. They were careful not to mass within range of the howitzers but they could be seen moving about for miles all around. Pinned there at Adobe Walls, the command could see groups of them returning to the village taken early that morning and carrying away valuables left before and rounding up again the horses and cattle "captured" by the scouts.

Hour after hour the battle continued unslacking, all the rest of the morning and on into the afternoon, and Assistant Surgeon Courtright was busy with the wounded in a corner of Adobe Walls and many a trooper regretted previous, hasty, slighting remarks about Father Kit's Utes and Apaches as they fought side by side with them in the tall grasses and the number of the enemy steadily increased and many and more dropped before the withering fire from the battle ring around the old ruins and still the number increased and Lieutenant Pettis saw what he had heard about and never quite believed and saw now in superb action. A shell from one of his howitzers drove straight through the body of a Comanche's horse to explode farther on and the horse crumpled and the man went sprawling, senseless on the ground, and as rifle balls from the troopers hummed over him two other Comanches dashed in at full gallop and swung down and each grabbed an arm and between them carried him to safety. And the battle continued and that kind of riding and rescue became a commonplace to Lieutenant Pettis's tired eyes, and all through the long hours someone among the enemy with a bugle mocked the orders given the troopers on the battle line by echoing each call with its opposite and the afternoon sun dropped down the sky to the west and Colonel Carson remembered that somewhere in this region alive with hostile Indians, back along the trail followed in the dark of the night and the first light of dawn, was his wagon train, whose loss would mean the almost inevitable destruction of his entire command. All that he had with him of food and ammunition beyond that carried by the men and already nearly spent was what had been brought along in the single light ambulance.

There were hotheads among the other officers who misread the fact that no direct massed frontal assault had been made by the enemy in the white man's manner and talked excitedly of hammering forward and taking the second village. Colonel Carson listened to them but wasted no time arguing with them. He ordered the supplies in the ambulance distributed and the wounded, those who still lived, loaded into it. He ordered the horses out from behind the ruined walls and into column by fours. He ordered each fourth man to ride leading three horses, the other men out as skirmishers front and flank, the howitzers and crew to act as rear guard. And he ordered the column into motion—backtracking the way they had come.

That was slow work, fighting every foot of the way, attacked from all sides, and the enemy set fire to the tall, winter-dried grasses and he had to show the men how to build backfires and swing them up along higher ground where the grasses were shorter and smoke clouds rolled over the column and warriors dashed in under their cover to fire almost point-blank and away and one of then was suddenly exposed by a breeze that swept aside the smoke and a young Mexican recruit among the troopers got him and dashed out and took the one scalp taken by the command that day and Lieutenant Pettis cursed that there were no targets visible for his howitzers and he and his men were all but useless again.

Not too long. The column broke through to the grazed-over, trodden space around the first village, that taken before, and Lieutenant Pettis rushed his guns up a small slope and they commanded the field again. There were warriors in the village fighting from among the lodges and shells dropped strategically drove them back, to the far edge, at last racing away, and the column moved in. The tired troopers were in retreat, yes, but they could do destruction as they went, and methodically they set to work to destroy the village and as dusk swept over the valley the fires of burning lodges fought briefly against it.

Night, and the enemy had pulled back in the darkness, a menace many thousand strong out around in the enveloping vastness. For thirty hours this striking force had been marching and fighting with little respite and nothing more than a teasing taste of raw bacon and hardtack, and the high hopes of the early morning were far and forgotten now and the wounded, suffering severely in the deepening cold, were loaded again on the ambulance and over the howitzers themselves on their carriages, and the remaining troopers swung into saddles and the column moved out again with Father Kit's Utes and Apaches scouting the path and the troopers willing now to let them, to depend on them, and the same thought beat in them all. Where and in what shape was the wagon train?

Captain Ahearn was an able, energetic yet cautious man and responsibility pressed hard upon him and he had slept little back there at Mule Spring. Twice during the night he had slipped out of his blankets and made a circuit of his pickets. He had the feeling, probably correct, that few of the men lying under and near the wagons were sleeping. Like him they were waiting, waiting their two-hour turns at guard and the morning that would send them forward on the trail of the striking force. In the grayness of first light, about the time the cavalry, miles on down the river, were splashing across and pursuing the first Kiowa pickets, he roused the camp and ordered a quick, hearty breakfast. That might be the last meal of many long hours. The situation, the responsibility, worried him. What kind of a commander was this Carson, so damned unmilitary, who could barely cipher out his own name in big childish letters, who had never studied military tactics in approved, formal manner, who never gave specific, detailed orders, just sweeping, wide-open commands and took for granted that those so commanded would know what to do and when and how to do it. The man had spent too many years up in the mountains with that bunch of wild-eyed, lawless trappers and hunters known as the Carson men, who could take right good care of themselves anytime anywhere with or without orders. He shouldn't be trusted with a batch of enlisted men who were used to having almost every minute of every day laid out for them and sometimes gave the impression they couldn't even blow their noses without instructions. If he did run into those Indians reported on up ahead, he'd probably let his men get scattered all over the whole country and the expedition would never be gathered together again.

Nonetheless Captain Ahearn noted that he missed the quiet, patient assurance of the man, that he felt remarkably alone and defenseless without it as a shield between him and the unknown ahead. And he missed too the once-scoffed-at screening protection of those screeching outlandish Utes and Apaches riding out on the flanks. Damn the man anyway, giving only the single sweeping order to come along in the morning—and the unspoken but understood implication to do whatever might need to be done along the way.

Captain Ahearn, able and cautious—which was why he was precisely where he was—had the wagons lashed tight, every strap tested as the teams were harnessed, every man's gun and cartridge box checked again, and formed his column, part of his infantrymen in front, others as flankers about two hundred yards out on the sides, within hailing distance, the remainder as rear guard, and in between the string of twenty-seven four-mule wagons.

They crawled forward, held to a foot pace, hour after hour, mile after mile, moving along the high, relatively-level ground north of the Canadian, following the trail of the cavalry, and dropped with it into the river valley and to its joining with the broad, beaten trail of the enemy. They tightened formation at this warning, this evidence of the actuality and nearness of menace, and moved on to the point where the cavalry had been discovered. The sun was high overhead now, edging into afternoon, and here they halted briefly and shed their heavy coats, tucking them under the lashings of the wagons, while Captain Ahearn pondered his decision. The scouts and most of the cavalry had crossed here, the fording plainly visible. Some of them and the battery and the light ambulance had kept on down the north side.

They moved on, following the wheel tracks, and the land was empty and silent around them and time passed and still the wheel tracks led on, and from far on out of sight ahead, whipped on wind up the valley, they heard the faint, dull booming of the howitzers and they quickened pace and the valley narrowed, the river deepening and swinging in to press them into a passageway not much more than two hundred feet wide between it and a high bluff cut by the flood waters of the centuries. Captain Ahearn felt the cold sweat of apprehension on his skin at the tight, trapping narrowness of the way and looked on forward and saw with relief the sharp ending of the bluff perhaps a half-mile ahead and the welcome, broadening, leveling-out of the valley beyond and leaped around startled at sudden shouts behind him. The whole column was stopping and the men of the rear guard were faced about, pointing, and he saw, back the way they had come, where the beginnings of the bluff dropped away to the valley level, the small, indistinct shapes of mounted men racing toward them. No troopers rode like that, weaving, formationless, a kind of remorseless wildness in the distant onrush, and the shock of realization struck through him and he saw with a sickening certainty that there were many of them and that some of them were swinging back to circle up around and come along the rim of the high overlooking bluff.

Damn and double damn the unmilitary colonel who would leave a fellow officer out in the middle of nowhere with wide-open orders and a batch of men who had to be told when to sneeze and would lead him along a string of wheel tracks into a squeeze like this. What would he himself do, caught on treacherous ground with a horde of howling Comanches on his tail?

Captain Ahearn found himself snapping orders, sending the whole column forward again on the double, shifting all but a single squad of his infantrymen to the rear, fanned out, hammering at his two top sergeants: "When they get within range, give 'em alternate volleys! Fire and fall back, goddamn it, fire and fall back! Get that through your goddamned, stinking, thick heads!" And trotting along near the lead wagons, neck stiffening from constant looking back, estimating distances in his mind, he began to feel better. He had a good start on those howling, cussed Comanches, particularly on those most dangerous, those who had cut back to come along the high bluff. Not much more and those would be temporarily out of it, stranded up there at the sharp end of the ridge, and he and the column would be out in the open with only those directly behind to worry about while they forted up with the wagons. And suddenly he realized that the column was stopping again, the wagons, one after another, jolting to a halt. Furious, unbelieving, he stopped too and glared ahead and saw what the forward squad had seen before him. There, just past the final narrowing at the bluff end, was a small, steep-sloped, stony hill, ridiculously small against the vastness of the open beyond, yet commanding, dominating, the passage. And clear against the sky on the top were three Indians waving and shouting to others who were leaping off horses below and climbing up and yet others were streaming into view, seen around the angle of the bluff end, dashing across the open toward that hill.

Captain Ahearn stood motionless a few seconds, caught in the shock of the seeming utter hopelessness of his position . . .

And up on the driver's seat of the first wagon a solid, compact, medium-sized man with the three ragged stripes of a sergeant on the sleeves of his work-worn jacket looked ahead from pulling his mule teams to a halt and saw the whole scene of which he was a single, small part, the whole enveloping situation, with a cold, logical clarity. This column, and with it the sustenance, the safety, the very existence of the entire command, was trapped; the river, unfordable here, on one side and a cliff on the other and the enemy behind and coming up above and blocking the passage ahead. And the only chance was to break through into the open and make a stand there behind the barricade of the wagons.

Quiet, steady, he looped the reins around the brake handle and took the rifle that was leaning against the seat between him and the man beside him and jumped out and to the ground and turned toward the second wagon.

"Fulton!"

Captain Ahearn told it to Major Pattison, weeks later, at Fort Union, earnest, blasphemous as always in excitement and monotonous and unimaginative in his blasphemy, trying by the very vehemence of his words to make the other understand what he himself, in sober afterthought, could not quite always believe had really happened that way.

"I'd heard about those goddamned pets of yours, Pat. Knew they were along. Had 'em pointed out. But I'd forgotten them. We'd been plugging along out there so goddamned long and they'd done their job without any goddamned fuss at all, they were just a bunch of teamsters to me. I had my own men to stew over, half of 'em getting bellyache and claiming the water was too goddamned alkali and such. Just a bunch of goddamned, stinking, mule-skinning teamsters! Do you get that, Pat? I'd forgotten they were anything else! And there we were, pegged in there! Couldn't fort up! Not there! Sure, we could stand off the devils down on our level! Those goddamned, bellyaching men of mine can shoot if they can't do a goddamned thing else! But soon as they came close up on top there, we'd be ducks in a barrel! Goddamned, stinking pigeons on a roost! I knew we'd have to bust out of there! But we'd have to clean 'em off that little hill first and keep 'em off! I was standing there sweating like a wet sponge somebody's squeezed, trying to figure how to make seventy-five men into twice as many and split 'em so to hold off in the rear while we busted ahead, and wondering did I have the goddamned, downright guts to send any of 'em up that goddamned, stinking, little hill! And that's when I heard it! The goddamnedest, silliest, craziest, finest sound I ever heard! Somebody up there by those front wagons was playing a mouth organ! A goddamned stinking little harmonica! May I roast ten thousand years in hell, Pat, but he was tootling out 'To Arms'! And those goddamned forgotten pets of yours were climbing down off their wagons and every single, solitary, god-damned one of them was lugging his rifle! And one of 'em, that Heath—goddamn it, Pat, I'll never forget that man! He comes straight to me and his eyes—goddamn it, Pat, ice! That's what they were! Ice! You'd think he was General Carleton himself! He says—get this, Pat—he says just like he was on parade ground somewhere giving orders to a young kid of a corporal—to me, Pat, goddamn it, with the bars standing out there on my shoulders— he says, 'Get some drivers on those wagons and keep 'em moving. We're taking that hill.' And he turns back to those others with me staring after him and he says, 'Fix bayonets' and they fix 'em and without another single, solitary, goddamned word he starts off toward that hill and every single, solitary, goddamned one of those pets right after him!"

They were under fire before they reached the upward slope and he saw Geary go down, no, up again clutching after his fallen rifle and dragging his right leg a bit and coming on, and they made it with a rush to the scant protection of the first of the boulders strewn up the slope and under the lash of his voice snapping in orders instinctive, unremembered, they began to work upward, fire in a volley at the rim of the hill above where the enemy lay hidden, unseen except in the glint of gun barrels poking over and the quick flash of a warrior rising with taut bow to send arrows humming downward, and dash forward to the next scant protection and crouch and rip open cartridges and load and fire again and dash forward again, upward, always upward.

He heard the guns of the squad at the head of the train go into action, below now and to the right, helping them, blocking a charge of mounted Indians attempting to sweep around the base of the hill and hit them from behind, and they drove upward and rock splinters from flying bullets scratched and tore at them and this was not an orderly, connected assault to be remembered as such but a series of glimpses caught and held: Selous, plump, panting, old Selous, shaking, shaking, feet stumbling, hands unsteady on rifle, making whimpering sounds in his throat, and firing and scrambling, crawling, clawing upward; Kinsey, leaping ahead, cap gone, hair flying, handsome face alight with a kind of fierce, released, mocking joy; Merriam, late, always late, moving out from each cover but always coming and with a frantic, dedicated rush; Fulton, small, quivering, breath drawing in quick tearing sobs, tears streaming down through the powder-black on his face, and loading and firing in jerky, spasmodic rhythm, and struggling, driving himself upward; Webb, stout, thickset, disdainful Webb, white-faced now, wide mustache startling against the white and black of his face, fumbling, having trouble loading, but coming, coming; Geary, pale, chewing on some sour anger, cursing steadily under his breath, straining forward and leaving sodden, dark marks where his right foot stepped; Zattig, seemingly calm, matter-of-fact, yet throwing back his head to bellow obscene answers to the derisive whoopings from above, and firing with swift, assured precision and leaping forward, big legs driving, and swinging over to throw a big arm around Geary and heave helping him to the next possible protection . . .

And somewhere up the slope: Merriam going down and staying down, crumpled behind the rock reached not quite in time, and somehow he himself was there, across the open between, crouched down looking into the face, young, unbelievably young, stripped of all the rushed, telescoped maturity of the last hard years, the eyes frightened, knowing, the life ebbing from them, and he saw the faint glimmer of pride struggle through and bent lower and caught the words, the final flicking of vitality. "It ain't in the foot, sir." And far back in his mind the harsh arithmetic of fact gave its total: seven.

And again, on up the slope: Webb suddenly jumping upright and dropping his rifle and running, running, headlong, desperate, down and down and away, and the thought hit him, yes, Webb would be the one, and he saw the stout figure jerk, head snapping from the smashing impact in the back, and fall sliding on down and far back in his mind the total clicked into consciousness: six.

They were well up now, only about thirty feet of bare, steep hillside between their last positions and the top, the angle of fire an asset for the moment, forcing the enemy to expose themselves to aim down. He crouched low behind jutting rock, sucking in great breaths to relieve the dry torment in his chest, waiting to let the others do the same, and he knew that the brief silence above meant the enemy were waiting too and he wondered without letting it be more than mere passing wonderment what those waiting above—seen first at a distance and since in the crowded, rushing moments only in partial glimpses through gunsmoke—really looked like and whether their number had been thinned. From back up the valley, beyond the train, he heard the crackle of gunfire as the rear guard loosed its first volley and then, suddenly, closer, much closer, the straining voice of Captain Ahearn. "Hold it, up there!"

He looked around and down and saw a dozen or more infantrymen at the base of the hill dropping into positions behind boulders and leveling rifles over them. And Captain Ahearn squatted behind one, making a megaphone of his hands.

"All right, you goddamned, stinking heroes! Lay low! We'll give you a barrage to shove 'em back some! Alternate fire! Four rounds! You keep count and go in hard after! Hold your own fire till you hit the top!"

He lay low, hugging the ground, and off to the right he heard the voice of Kinsey, soft, gently mocking. "Zattig, you bumptious, big ape. I'll lay you a five-spot out of any pay we ever get I beat you up there." And Zattig's low rumble was lost in the first volley from below and the infantrymen down there hammered on, half firing while the others loaded, good men with their guns, able to make it four shots in sixty seconds, eight volleys from them in the single moment, and dirt flew in spurts from the upper rim of the hill, and hard after he pushed up and led out for the last plunging rush to the top. Out on the fleeting edge of vision he saw Geary struggle to rise and fall back and the harsh arithmetic hummed in his mind, five, and he drove on and someone or something struck him savagely in the side under the left shoulder and spun him partway around and he wondered vaguely what it was and had no time for wondering because he was driving on, legs pumping against the steepness, and sharp against the sky above and to the right he saw the tall, graceful figure of Kinsey and close beside it the huge shape of Zattig leaping over the top edge, rifles spurting flame, and plowing forward with the sun glinting on the bright steel of their bayonets, and he broke over the top too and through the pulsing, wild yells sweeping around him he heard from behind and to the left the sobbing of young Fulton and the whimpering of old Selous, coming on, coming on, and in the one swift glance he took in the small, fairly level space of the hilltop. Five bodies lay there, dirty, coppery in color, naked except for moccasins and manhood strings at the waists and strange paint streaks and lone feathers twisted into the dark hair, one of them still feebly moving, crawling toward the other edge, and nine more, short, powerful demons possessed, leaping, yelling, converging on Kinsey and Zattig. The thought flitted across his mind that there might have been more and he heard, coming from below on around toward the other side, the sound of gunfire and he knew. Some of those blessed infantrymen were keeping them busy around there. And two of them were rushing at him, dropping emptied guns, and one had a knife and the other a hatchet and it struck him strange that the hatchet should be exactly like one he had used on kindling as a boy and he shifted the muzzle of his rifle and fired and that one faded from in front of him and he swung the rifle up parrying the blow of the other with the knife and had to concentrate on the effort because his left arm was curiously weak and he swung the bayonet on, cutting across the man's face, blinding him with blood, and he had to turn sideways and brace his left elbow against his hip to hold the bayonet steady for the forward, plunging stroke. The body of the man falling wrenched the weapon from his hands and he stumbled forward, grasping it, pulling to free it, and another of them was rushing at him and a gun blazed a few feet away and the man crumpled sideways and Fulton staggered past him, breath a sobbing rattle in his throat, and he pulled at the gun and it came free with a jerk dripping blood across his feet and he saw Selous, shaking, shaking, unable to stand, crawling up over the near edge and struggling to his knees and to raise his rifle and firing across the level space and suddenly, hard after the sharp crack of the shot, there was a silence, an absence of sound on the hilltop. Swaying, aware at last of the warm wetness soaking his jacket, he turned and saw two of them dropping in flight over the other edge and turning on he saw Fulton and Zattig standing quiet staring down and in the tangle of bodies at their feet the limp figure of Kinsey, that smile of fierce, mocking joy frozen forever on his face, and the feathered shaft of the arrow protruding from his neck, and the harsh arithmetic of fact clicked again in his mind, four, and turning on he saw, straining weakly over the near edge, the head and shoulders of Geary, blood dripping from his chin from underlip bitten through the clenched teeth, the eyes fixed on him, calling, pleading. He swayed over and dropped to his knees and reached with his right arm to help and the head shook feebly and the teeth unclenched and he bent lower and saw the effort summoning the last trace of strength and the torn lips move. "I wasn't running away. I was looking for them." And his mind leaped back across the months and the miles to a small, isolated woodlot in northern Virginia. "Yes," he said softly. "Yes, I know." And he did not even have the certainty that the man heard as the life guttered out, and he raised his head and as he knelt there on a small hilltop in the far

Southwest looking into the distances of this vast, stripped, strong land the hard rock of his being shattered and fell apart and reformed, firmer, harder than before, and he rose swaying to his feet to do what still needed to be done, to post his remaining men along the other edge to hold the hill, and below he saw the wagon train moving, moving on past toward the open level of the broadened valley and infantrymen out in a skirmish line ahead and beside it and others of them coming up the hill toward him, near the top now, calling to him. The rifle fell from his left hand and he wondered why there was no strength in the fingers and a red mist floated across his vision and something struck him across the back and he realized he was on the ground and just as the curtain of blackness closed he saw through the thickening mist the huge shape of Zattig bending down.

Seven

He was awake and aware that he was awake in a great darkness and gradually his eyes focused on far points of light and he knew that they were stars and that he lay on the ground in the night, a folded blanket under his head, another stretched over him. A numbness held his left side and he tried to move and darting pains through the numbness warned against that. Carefully he rolled his head to the right and saw the blunt, darker shape of a wagon. Carefully he rolled his head to the left and saw, against the dim glow of what must be a small fire well beyond, the big, hunched figure squatted within reach if he could reach, knees drawn up and arms clasped around them.

"Zattig," he said and was surprised at the weak whispering of his own voice.

The big head swung toward him. "I was thinkin' ye'd never say that agin. Ye been out a long time, Sarge."

"What happened?"

"Ye got pretty well smashed there, Sarge. The ball's still in ye somewheres. An' ye had an arrow in yer arm."

"I mean after that."

"Nothin' much. Them territory boys corraled the wagons out

here an' we brung everybody in. Them painted devils rode around like crazy darin' us to fight but we stuck close an' they stuck pretty well out a range an' along about sundrop they all went scutterin' off downriver."

He lay quiet, thinking back. "Fulton? And Selous?"

"Sleepin' now, Sarge. They was done in. But they made it down here, helpin' carry. Helped dig too."

"Dig?"

"For the others, Sarge. We buried 'em. The cap'n's orders. We didn't know when ye would come out a it. An' we had to get it done with. Might have to move soon as we know what's doin' with the cav'lry. He gave 'em a full company salute, Sarge. An' Fulton gave 'em taps."

He lay quiet, trying to hold to what he had heard, and drifting away, and the low voice, rumbling in the big throat, caught him. "It like to a killed him. Fulton. But he got through it. An' then he dropped that little tune thing down in there . . . With Kinsey . . . Wish I'd a had a five-spot to put in there too . . . He was a hard one to take but he was a good man . . . Kinsey . . ."

"All of them were, Zattig." If only he could get more strength into his voice. "All of them."

"Even Webb? Mebbe . . . in a way. I figger mebbe he come further'n he ever did before . . . But I know what I know, Sarge. Kinsey was up there on his own. An' mebbe Geary. But the others, them that's dead an' them that's livin' too, you was pullin' 'em up that hill, Sarge, pullin' 'em, makin' 'em do it with what ye been puttin' into 'em since that first day back in Virginny . . ."

And he should be speaking, driving into the man that all he had done was a job that was his to do and with whatever means came to hand and the finest of these had been a big, slab-sided ex-sergeant and whatever had taken them up that hill with him was inalienably theirs, each his own, and he could not speak and he lay quiet and was drifting away into the far darkness when the low voice caught him again.

"I can't figger it, Sarge. A big hulkin' thing like me. Ye'd think I'd be easy hit. An' I never get nicked. An' look at Kinsey, who weren't half as wide. An' thin little Geary—ye didn't know he was hit twicet, did ye? Oncet in the leg, which didn't nip bone but must a bled bad, an' agin in the gut. An' that sawed-off, little shorty Merriam..."

Silence except for the hushed rustling of movements elsewhere in the circled camp and he could sense, because it was the same for him, the big man beside him grasping the fact not alone that these men were dead but that what had been was broken and that out here in the lonesomeness of the great distances a shared road had reached an ending...

"I figger," said Private Hugo Zattig, "this jist about winds up Company Q."

"Yes," he said. "Yes. I expect it does..."

"Me now," said Private Zattig. "I figger I'll be puttin' in for me discharge. Back to Indianny. There's a wife an' a couple a kids waitin'. Ye didn't know that, did ye, Sarge?"

"No," he said. "No, I didn't." And he lay quiet, drifting in the darkness with the thought that he had known nothing, that he knew nothing, of the personal, secret lives of any of them, that in some tacit, not even realized, understanding they had not shared this and had been right not to share it because circumstances had removed them from it, each in his own lonely, individual isolation which only, the loneliness and the isolation and the long movement toward the ultimate sharing of an advance up a small, rocky hillside, had been theirs to share. And then one word out of those spoken struck him.

"Discharge?" he said.

"That's right, Sarge. Me last hitch run out about six weeks back."

He tried to move, disregarding the darting fingers of pain, to rise up, to turn toward the man, and a big hand clamped him to the ground.

"Easy, Sarge. Don't go pullin' at that hole . . . I made up me mind. Did ye think I'd let the rest a ye keep goin' an' me not with ye?"

The effort to push up had drained him of strength and he lay quiet, drifting in and out of a deeper darkness, and a stirring ran through the camp and the sound of hurrying feet and the far-off jingle of metal and the big figure beside him rose, moving away in long, loose-jointed stride, and time passed and the figure was there again, crouching close. "The cav'lry's found us an' comin' in." And it was gone again and time passed and voices made a clamor everywhere that beat at him, irritating, meaningless, and he tried to drift away and suddenly was back, caught by the known voice rumbling in a big throat somewhere near. "Over here, sir." And another voice, tired, exasperated: "Can't it wait till morning? I've had a day." And then the voice of Captain Ahearn: "Goddamn it, Courtright! You'll take care of that man right now if I have to put a goddamned, stinking gun in your back!" And men crowded around and one carried a lantern and another a pail from which steam rose in the lantern light and Assistant Surgeon Courtright was kneeling beside him, lifting away the blanket, spreading open the jacket, removing the improvised bandage, swabbing raw flesh, and the fingers of pain raced and grew and as the steel probe entered merged into the one blinding, rocking agony and he flung out his right arm and clutched a big ankle and gripped and clung and as he rushed into the welcome blankness he heard the tired, exasperated voice saying: "Got it."

Early morning, just before daybreak, and Colonel Carson had the command up and posted to repel an attack and there was no attack. The sun tipped over the horizon eastward down the valley and there was not an enemy in sight. Breakfast and the camp settled to a day of rest and recuperation and there was a flurry of excitement when some of the enemy were sighted on a low, long ridge several miles away and these remained in view all through the day and Colonel Carson knew they were there as a reminder, a warning, against any attempt at another advance toward their winter villages, and his men rested and caught up on their meals and Assistant Surgeon Courtright was busy with the wounded, twenty-one cavalrymen and several infantrymen and some of the Utes and a man named Jared Heath.

Another night and morning again and most of the officers, still misreading the facts of the fighting, misunderstanding the day of quiet, wanted to push on and attack the big village beyond Adobe Walls. Colonel Carson argued a little with them and then paid them no more attention. He talked with his Utes and his Apaches, squatting to listen to those who had slipped like shadows out in the night and back in the darkness before dawn, and what they said, what they advised, confirmed what he knew in his aging, Indian-wise bones, that thousands of determined warriors were just beyond the low, encircling horizon, that not a move was made in his camp without their swift knowledge of it, that only his howitzers and the concentrated, forted strength of his camp kept them from an overwhelming assault. They had stopped him, started him into retreat, and for the present were reluctantly content with that. If he should push on they would fight and fight and steadily wear his force down, run him eventually out of ammunition, besiege him constantly, and the ultimate result was certain. As long as he had luck and those howitzers and kept his strength concentrated and in readiness they might let him backtrack to safety. To push on would be simply to reissue a challenge, to move further into a deadly trap . . . He gave his orders and the cavalry saddled and the mule teams were harnessed and the command started the long trailing westward toward Fort Bascom, held tight together with flankers always in force, moving slowly, swinging up out of the valley to stay on the high, wide-open levels. And left behind back down the valley at Adobe Walls were graves deliberately hidden, obliterated against defilement by the passage of cavalry and gun carriages over them, and more just outside the ruined Kiowa village, and four more where the wagon train had corraled.

And midway in the moving train now was the remnant of Company Q, one wagon, four men, a slender young one on the driver's seat who no longer slouched, sunk within himself, but sat erect, the reins in his hands, and beside him a plump, late-middle-aged second with a short, square-cut beard who again and again climbed over into the partially emptied bed of the wagon to arrange and rearrange buffalo robes from the burned, looted Kiowa village as cushions against the jolting for the limp, unconscious figure of the third, and behind, keeping pace in long, loose-jointed stride by the tailgate, the big, thick-chested, flat-shanked fourth.

He drifted in and out of consciousness as the days went under the rolling wheels and his body was incredibly weak against the punishment of the jolting and that meant nothing because strong soups made with wild turkey and antelope meat brought in by the scouts were working in him and deep in the marrow of the bones in his solid, compact body new blood was forming and moving out through him and in the increasing moments of consciousness his mind was clear and calm and there was no pressure of tensions in him, only an enduring quietness. At times he felt his lips moving a bit, shaping into a grim, ironic smile at the fussy solicitude of Selous and at the snap in the voice of Fulton urging the mules on and as he looked up at the endless, limitless, blue vaulting of the sky he found himself thinking of this land not consciously noted, assessed, understood in the strain of the outward journey, not seen now from low in the wagon except in the miracle of the sky overhead, yet remembered, clearly, in effect, in feeling, this land stripped and sparse and bare and strong and challenging and harsh and arid that offered so little in prospect of profit and comfort and easy closeness of crowded living and yet gave so much in the summoning strength of its distances and the serene, indifferent beauty of its stretching, golden, winter-cured plains and raw-colored, eroded hillsides and the far, beckoning, immovable majesty of its mountains.

And now and again, in the first days, when he emerged into consciousness, he was aware of one or more of the scouts, black-haired, black-eyed, strong-featured faces inscrutable to him, peering at him from over the tailgate, and nodding at the awareness rising in his own eyes, and speaking, strange, unintelligible, and suddenly across the barrier of race reaching him with a personal warmth, and moving away, and he did not know, not then, that they were marking him in memory, known to them as Man-Who-Climbs-the-Hill, that if ever in the long progress of the years his path should touch theirs again he should walk in peace and in honor among them.

And every evening as the days slid into weeks, right after mess and Zattig had brought him food and had lifted him out of the wagon for the inconvenient necessities of existence and had lifted him back again, Captain Ahearn appeared and said, always the same and always in the same tone that meant the opposite of the words: "Mutiny. That's what it was. Mutiny. Giving me orders. Goddamn it, man, I ought to prefer charges."

And once, at midday, when they had stopped to water the horses and mules, a smallish, wiry, droopy-mustached man looked in with eyes the same clear, clean, cold blue of the winter sky and said: "I bin wonderin', boy. Whar was you raised?" He heard himself answer: "Massachusetts." And a wry grin twitched the sandy mustache and the man said, "Wal-l-l, now, I'll be shook," and raised a hand in a queer, unmilitary salute and was gone about the tiring, tiresome business of herding the command on out of dangerous territory.

And every day, for the first week, sometime through the hours Indians would be sighted on some distant ridge, a reminder, a warning, and then no more were seen and the column moved on across the Llano Estacado and on across the wide vegas of eastern New Mexico and most of December rolled under the slow wheels and a few days before Christmas the lonely, timeless landmark of Tucumcari rose out of the horizon to the southwest, and by late afternoon they dropped down to the river and recrossed where they had crossed six weeks before and to Fort Bascom.

Two days there with the wagon his quarters and in the release from the jolting he began to experiment with the muscles of his left arm, flexing them gently and feeling the strength creeping into them, and he had Selous slip a rolled buffalo robe under his shoulders so he could have his head up and look about some and on the second day Captain Clark stood by the wagon scowling at him and behind the scowling an embarrassment, a searching for words, and said: "So you fixed me, didn't you. Now I'll have to break in another brickmaking crew . . . Ahearn's taking you on to Union. If Pattison doesn't treat you right just spit in his eye and come back this way." And Captain Clark lifted a hand in a neat, precise, very military salute and was gone . . . out of his life, out of the existence he was leaving.

Christmas on the trail to Fort Union and that was just another day except for going into camp earlier than usual to have a good meal before dark of wild turkey roasted over hot coals and by New Year's Day he was comfortable on a cot in the hospital that stood apart from the wide, rectangular layout of the other buildings of the big headquarters post. He was able to sit up now and he sat up against a straw-stuffed pillow when Major Pattison limped in and stood staring down at him.

"Heath. I've got it all. From Captain Ahearn. Sounds funny, I suppose, seeing there's dead men involved in this, but I want to say I'm grateful. Pattison's pets. I won't mention names but I've been able to make certain people around here eat those words . . . Now I've got to send some kind of report back East. Nothing about you and your men goes through regular channels. Just dumped on me. You know how it is, let Pattison do it. All right, Pattison'll do it. And I've got it. Just one thing I want from you. One statement . . . Did all of them come through for you?"

He leaned back, not alone against the softness of a straw-stuffed pillow but against the enduring support of the quietness within him. "Yes," he said. "Yes. All of them. Not separate men. Company Q."

Major Pattison stared down at the brick floor, apparently fascinated by the pattern of the lines there. He leaned over slightly and began to massage his game leg. He straightened. "Very well,

Heath. That's the way it will be . . . Holler for good service here if you have to, it's coming to you. And don't worry about the three men you have left. Pattison'll take care of them . . ."

And the days slipped one into another and Zattig swung the cot around for him and raised it on some bricks so he could look out one of the windows at the remote, rising ridges of the Sangre de Cristo in the lonely, lifting distances and the post surgeon grunted and let that ride and in the evenings until just before taps the three of them would be there with him and the hospital steward frowned and let that ride too, Selous on a stool beside the cot playing checkers with him and Zattig squatted on the floor puffing on a pipe acquired somewhere, probably from Major Pattison's collection, and pushing sly questions at Fulton stretched near and writing, writing, seemingly endless letters all to the same person and poring over them with the silly, ridiculous, magnificent, hopeful half-smile of youth.

The crushed, torn muscles of his left side under the shoulder knit and strengthened and he could be on his feet and moving about between restings on the cot and late one morning Zattig appeared, standing enormous at the foot of the cot, chipped rock of broad face flat and expressionless. "Don't ye move, Sarge. There's a train leavin' for the States an' I'm goin' with it. I got me discharge this mornin' an' at me old ratin'. An' what's that? Jist a scrap a paper. I got somethin' better inside me an' ye gave it to me. There ain't no need a words atween us so I'm shuttin' me yap. I got to go an' I'm goin'." And Zattig too was gone . . . gone as so many others were gone who had known him, whom he had known, on the long way from a small town in Massachusetts through the tangled, matted Wilderness in northern Virginia to the great, spreading reaches of this old, new land . . .

And a few days later, in the afternoon, Selous and Fulton

appeared and said they were wanted, the three of them, at Major Pattison's quarters and they helped him put on his jacket and he went with them, leaning on Fulton, over to the other buildings, past the troop barracks, along the line of officers' row houses to the last unit. And as he stood under the wide portal by the doorway a familiar feeling of inevitability was upon him and he straightened, away from Fulton, erect, on his own . . .

"Sit down, gentlemen, there are chairs enough," said Major Pattison from the padded comfort of his own, pleased, very pleased with himself, tapping a folded paper against his game leg. He surveyed them, seated. "Jesu Becky! Pattison's pets! . . . Well, Pattison has been doing some petting. The department dumped you on me with instructions to report anything worth reporting. Jesu Becky Maria! What a way to do things! Well, I reported and I laid it on the line and I demanded, downright demanded, appropriate action and I got it. Don't know just how the department's handling it because I gather they're not keeping any permanent record of this Company Q business. Too damned irregular. But they're straightening out individual records all right . . ."

Major Pattison looked directly at him, singling him out, pleased, triumphant. "The four who got killed out there, all the same. Previous convictions set aside. Commissions restored as of day of death."

Major Pattison transferred the folded paper to the other hand and began to massage his thigh. You all know about Zattig . . . Fulton! You're the one tootled that dimdamned harmonica, aren't you? You're going back to your regiment. They've been shot up bad and need men. Subaltern, weren't you? Well, you're going back a full lieutenant. Skip along now over to the quartermaster. I've talked to him and he'll fix you up best he can with a decent uniform . . . Jesu Becky Maria Sanctissima! Don't sit there looking silly! Get along. And don't worry about these other two. Pattison's taking care of them."

Major Pattison watched young Fulton disappear out the doorway and bent over to massage farther down the leg, head cocked at an angle to look up. "Selous. Your regiment's been about knocked out. It'll probably be combined with a couple others in the same fix. Captain, weren't you? Well, your commission's waiting for you again back East and they'll fit you into the outfit all right . . . Jesu Becky, man! What's the matter? Isn't that what you wanted?"

"That's what I want," said old Selous, square-cut beard quivering and fighting that and the shakiness of his voice with strange, stiffening dignity. "I earned that commission once and certainly I want it back. But a man has to face up to things. I go to pieces. I went to pieces out there again and I'd of been running like—well, I'd of been running, only there was a goddamned, heartless bastard of a better man than me out there too who wouldn't let me run. I found out I could follow him. But I couldn't have led anyone into it. Knowing that, I can't let them make me a line officer again. It wouldn't be fair to the men under me."

Major Pattison stopped rubbing his leg and stared at Selous. He closed his eyes for a moment and drew in a long breath. "Jesu Becky Maria, man! It strikes me it takes as much downright-be-damned guts to say something like that as to go whooping into any battle! Don't be so all-fired-furious finicky! Just be like everybody else around here and let Pattison fix it. You're no young sprout anyway. I'll send along a recommendation they give you a spot in the supply division. They need men there too. I understand they're going crazy trying to give Grant all the stuff he wants . . . All right, all right, man, Pattison's used to fixing things. That's all he's good for nowadays. Trot along over to the quartermaster who's waiting for you and leave this—this heartless bastard here. I've a few things to say to him."

Major Pattison watched old Selous depart and straightened on his chair, leaning back, pleased, very pleased with himself and not in any patronizing manner but in the simple, honest knowledge that he had been able to do what he thought, what he knew, was the right, the decent, thing to do and that the knuckleheads in the War Department had had the rare sense to agree with him.

"Heath. It's the way you wanted it. All the same. Your commission has been restored. But it's not waiting for you back East. It's on its way out here. I didn't know at the time, but the colonel sent a note along with my report. I think Ahearn filled his ear. And he has his troubles what with so many good men pulled out of the territory. He wants you on his staff . . . But that's left open. You can go back East if you want. Your regiment went out of existence months ago but they'll give you a company in another. Or you can stay here where there's damn-good chances of being breveted up . . . It is your choice."

Gently Major Pattison tapped his left leg with the folded paper, pleased, very pleased. And in a few seconds he was no longer pleased . . .

It is there in his copybook, the longest passage in the pages, the baffled, honest confession of a man confronted with something beyond his comprehension. Perhaps not beyond it but outside it, because he did not know except in a few bare, meaningless facts what had happened across the miles and the months before that day in August when eight odd-sized scarecrows came into his quadrangle toward him.

I felt like a fool. I was giving that man what I will never have for myself again—and not one chance but two—a choice—two chances—to be back in the swing again, an officer on the way up. His record wiped clean and two chances to go on and gather more glory for himself and the service. The look of him—the—the feel of him—I would have said he was the best chunk of man to put into an officer's uniform I had ever laid eyes upon. He had taken those others the army chucked aside and made them into men who would follow him straight into hell—and did into something like it. I would have said he could do the same with any bunch of men you could scrape together. I would have said if I was younger, leg or no leg, I would serve under that man myself—I gave him his chances. He just smiled a funny little smile that was not at me—at something way past me somewhere. He just said: No. Neither one. I am not good officer material.

Not officer material!

All right—if there is some crazy quirk in him that does not show—and I do not believe it—I will not believe it—let him say that. What licks me—what I cannot get at—he was happy about it. Happy! It just did not worry him at all—

Then he said just as if he were stating a fact about the weather—and I remember every word—he said: I've paid my debts. To everyone. And to the army. I'm a three-year man and I've served well past three years and since I haven't accepted that commission again I'm still in the ranks. That makes me eligible for a discharge. A discharge! That man! Then he just froze on that chair—hard like a rock—and his eyes—just like Ahearn told me—ice—He said: All I want from the army is a quit claim, complete and final.

That made me mad the way it would anybody decent who feels he ought to be in uniform doing his share in times like this. I tried

to shame him and said something about he would likely grab at all
the back pay he could get. He just looked at me—not angry or
upset just the way he was at first. He said: No. If the army will
give me a horse and a rifle, I'll call it even. Anything over can go
in the post fund.

So we sat there looking at each other—me feeling like a fool—
and he was not hard anymore just quiet and—I guess the only
word for it is quiet—not just silent—quiet—and immovable—
like one of those mountains over by Santa Fe. Then he said not
sarcastic or mean but sort of reaching to me: Pattison can do it.
And he smiled that funny little smile but this time at me—and for
a moment there I knew why those men followed him—

I knew too I never wanted to see that man again—not even
hear about him. But he had something—he had got hold of some-
thing—I wish I knew what it was—what made him so quiet—
chucking a commission away—a man with two good legs—And I
knew he had used me once and he was using me again—but—
but—I said I would do it.

And when the next wagon train pulled out on the old trail north
and east Selous and Fulton were gone too and more days slipped
one into another and he slept on the cot pushed now into a corner
of the big hospital room and took meals with the hospital mess
and he was, as he had been from a day in late spring looking out
over a bright green valley in Virginia, a marked man, only now no
one bothered him, the men of the post respecting what they had
heard of a hillside in Comanche country and his quiet withdrawal
here, and few came near him except an occasional private confined
to the hospital, careful in conversation with him, playing checkers
with him, and he spent long hours sitting outside in the sun and
walking out into the beckoning distances and the muscles down

his left side under the shoulder strengthened more and healed and the sun and the endless wind of the high country tanned his face and one morning an orderly appeared and handed him an envelope and said: "The rest of it's outside."

He opened the envelope and took out a single piece of paper, an honorable discharge for a Sergeant Jared Heath. He picked up the jacket, from which he had long since removed all markings and put it on and took from a pocket a small, leather-laced account book and folded the piece of paper and tucked it between the pages and put the small, worn book back into the pocket. He took his cap and put it on and went to the door. Outside, ground-reined, patient, waiting, was a medium-sized, solidly muscled, dark bay horse, saddled, and a rifle in the scabbard and a cartridge box hanging by a long leather loop. He took the cartridge box and slipped the loop over his head to hang on his right shoulder with the box at his left side and swung up into the saddle.

Quiet, steady, he rode out around the hospital and angled past the buildings of the fort and the few men who saw him turned to watch him go and one of them, standing by the transportation corrals, leaned against the rails to favor a stiff right leg and he turned slightly in the saddle toward this one and raised a hand in a salute, the last he would ever give and not to the uniform, to the rank, but to the man, and he headed off across the great golden plain that was touched now with the first faint, green flush of returning spring toward the far, rising foothills of the mountains.

He had the clothes he wore and a horse and a rifle. Only those. And something more. An enduring quietness within. He rode west, a man akin to the great timeless mountains that he would see marching in their own majestic, indifferent serenity along the horizon of his small homestead ranch all the rest of his days.

Author's Note

Perhaps it is necessary, at least advisable, to state here that Jared Heath and his rag-tail Company Q had no existence, have no existence, outside the pages of this book. They are figures out of history only in the tenuous sense that each, in barest-broad outline of character and in the action which led to conviction of cowardice, was drawn from an actual Civil War court-martial case or group of cases. In each instance, starting with a specific type of "cowardly" act, checking records of convictions for such an act, I tried to create a man, a human personality, who might have committed that act.

Only Jared Heath, of course, is sketched in with fair fullness. And that is right because this is his story. It is true that Company Q, the notion of a book about a Company Q, came first. But I had rejected that, was turning away from it—and the man himself took over in my mind and insisted that his story be told.

A book like this is, again of course, a deliberate and to some people irritating mixture of fact and fiction. A simple rule of thumb of separating fact from fiction is this: Jared Heath, his acts, the people (except for Kit Carson and Assistant Surgeon Courtright) with whom he comes in contact, and their acts, though all derived from study of actual people and actual happenings of the period and always fitted into a framework of what could have been, are wholly fictional. Everything else in the book, including and emphasizing the battle at Adobe Walls, is as true to recorded history as I have been able to make it.

The reason for the original rejection of the Company Q notion makes a curious small tale in itself.

On page 215 of *A Stillness at Appomattox*, published in 1953, Bruce Catton stated:

> For a time the 150th Pennsylvania contained a unique detachment known as "Company Q," made up of line officers from other regiments who had been court-martialed and broken for cowardice but who were given the chance to serve as private soldiers and, if they could, redeem themselves. Company Q turned out to be a good fighting unit, and most of the men ultimately regained their commissions.

Very good. Very interesting. Certainly a provocative passage, stirring the imagination storyward. But if any story, based on that, were to have some semblance of authenticity, in background at least, more facts were needed. An inquiry to the National Archives brought the following reply from Dr. Richard G. Woods, chief of the Old Army Section:

> An examination of the records of the Adjutant General's Office (Record Group 94) in the National Archives including rosters, regimental returns and Company hooks of the 150th Pennsylvania Volunteers, has failed to disclose any information pertaining to a Company "Q," attached to the 150th Pennsylvania Volunteers.

If you can furnish us with the names of any of the individuals
belonging to this Company another search will be made. ,

Not so good. Where, then, did Bruce Catton get his information? According to his Notes, from a *History of the One Hundred and Fiftieth Regiment, Pennsylvania Volunteers* by a Lieutenant Colonel Thomas Chamberlin, published in 1895. A copy of that was hard to locate out in the wide-open spaces of northern New Mexico, but at last one was found, the 1905 revised edition. On pages 239–240 it stated:

> The discipline and standing of the 150th are brought into high relief by the fact that several line-officers from other organizations, whose valor had been badly shaken by repeated conflicts, were sent, stripped of the insignia of their rank, by sentence of drum-head court-martial, and provided with the arms and accoutrements of private soldiers, to share the fortunes of the regiment and redeem, if possible, their clouded reputations. Major Jones was quietly instructed to keep them in the "forefront of battle" and maintain a close watch of their conduct, as upon his report, after a given time, would depend their dismissal from the army or their restoration to their former places. This unique squad joined the 150th on the 13th day of May (1864) and was known as "Company Q." It is a pleasure to state that in subsequent engagements all of these delinquents acquitted themselves so creditably that they were eventually permitted to return to their old commands.

No names of individual members there. But more information, even an exact date and the name of the officer instructed to report on them. A copy of that passage was sent to Dr. Woods. His reply was definite if not definitive.

> An examination of the records of the Department of the Army in the National Archives has failed to disclose any information concerning any unit or organization officially designated as Company Q or any individuals of the character described in your letter assigned, attached, or associated with the 150th Pennsylvania Infantry.
>
> With respect to the possibility of such disposition of commissioned officers during this period, reference may be made to *Revised United States Army Regulations, 1863.*

No good at all. The national research outfit, patient and always obliging, with access to all available official records, which can even turn up the name and ultimate disposition of a specific army mule on request, could find no trace of a Company Q. And a careful check of all pertinent sections of the 1863 revised regulations made it plain that the very concept of a Company Q was contrary to those regulations and that such a company could have been created only by some deliberate relaxing of them on very high authority indeed.

Two possible conclusions seemed logical. Lieutenant Colonel Chamberlin was right and there had been a Company Q but the War Department, because of the irregularity and uniqueness of the procedure, kept no official record of it. Or there had been no Company Q, only an apocryphal postwar legend, and Lieutenant Colonel Chamberlin, writing his book thirty years after the war, citing all conceivable evidence of "the discipline and standing" of the regiment, simply took for granted it was founded in fact and included it.

Of the two, the second seemed to me the more likely because my own research, though certainly not exhaustive, disclosed only a few, a very few, other references to Company Q—and each of these was written after 1895 and could within reason be traced to the Chamberlin book.

So I rejected the notion of a Company Q, a book about a Company Q. And meantime a man named Jared Heath had taken hold of my mind and was insisting that his story be told. And after a while, as he emerged from the Battle of the Wilderness and faced the consequences of his act, he demanded, the emerging pattern of his story demanded, that he be given a company, a Company Q. So I gave it to him—in the only way, on the only scale, handled in the only manner, accorded the only treatment, which seemed to me consistent with the time and the circumstances and what I had learned of the administration of military justice in the Civil War years.

Jack Schaefer
Cerrillos Flats
March, 1957